Y

Summer Secrets

by Patricia Hermes

Marshall Cavendish

New York   London   Singapore

For Laurrie McClain Hermes

Marshall Cavendish Children's Books
Marshall Cavendish
99 White Plains Road
Tarrytown, NY 10591
www.marshallcavendish.com

Text copyright © 2004 by Patricia Hermes

Library of Congress Cataloging-in-Publication Data
Hermes, Patricia.
Summer secrets /c by Patricia Hermes.– 1st ed.
p. cm.
Summary: Twelve-year-old Missy tries to learn more about her mother's
odd behavior as she and her two friends share some secrets during a
long, hot summer in Mississippi toward the end of World War II.
ISBN 0-7614-5074-2
[1. Mental illness–Fiction. 2. Friendship–Fiction. 3. Family
problems–Fiction. 4. Race relations–Fiction. 5.
Mississippi–History–20th century–Fiction. 6. World War,
1939-1945–United States–Fiction.] I. Title.
PZ7.H4317Su 2004
[Fic]–dc22
2003017669

Book design by Anahid Hamparian
The text of this book is set in New Baskerville.

Printed in the United States of America
First edition
6 4 2 1 3 5 7

O_{ne}

$\mathcal{M}$*ama is acting different again.*

No. If I'm going to tell this story, I'm going to tell the truth. Mama is acting crazy. Again.

I wouldn't *say* that, but I can write it in my secret notebook. Mama is crazy. For a long time now, this whole past spring, I've tried hard not to notice. When she did strange things, I'd think—well, that's all right. Strange things aren't always crazy. Even last week, when she cut all the buttons off all of Daddy's shirts to feed them to the birds—well, so what? Daddy didn't seem to mind. He didn't make a big fuss about it, just asked Geneva if she could find new buttons and sew them on for him. So if Daddy didn't worry, why should I? And then the day she gave all of her clothes to the ragman— well, maybe she just wanted a whole new wardrobe. Daddy bought it for her, too.

So those things were sort of weird. But not crazy—I don't think. Mama is different, always has been, but fun different. She's always been more like my best friend than my mama. Geneva is more like my mama. Only once, a long time ago, Mama got so different—all right, crazy—that she had to go away. But for years now, she's been better.

But then today happened, and I can't pretend any longer that it's just "different."

It was early this morning at breakfast time, when Mama came sidling up to Daddy. She was all dolled up, smelling of that lavender water she uses, but she looked nervous, her eyes darting back and forth, her fingers twitching at the neck of her blouse.

"Sweets?" she said. She leaned into Daddy's shoulder. "I need something."

"What is it, dear one?" Daddy said. "What do you need?"

"Ribbons," Mama said. "Lots of them. All colors. Will you? I know you got new ones at the store yesterday."

"Oh, you know that, do you?" Daddy said, smiling.

Mama nodded. "Maureen told me," she said.

Daddy shook his head, still smiling. "She would. That bookkeeper of mine would rob me blind. And what kind of ribbons would you like?" he asked.

"Pretty ones!" Mama said. "The prettiest ones you have."

Daddy pulled her close. He tipped her face up to his and kissed her nose and Mama snuggled against him. I love watching them when they're like this, Mama being sweet and nice and kind, Daddy holding her close. Sometimes, they both turn to me at times like that, holding out their arms, and then we have a family hug. But now, even though Mama was wrapped in Daddy's arms, I noticed that her eyes were still doing that nervous kind of thing, darting side to side, anxious-like. Suddenly, she pulled away from Daddy and spun around, her eyes fixed on me.

"What is it?" Daddy asked.

For a long minute, Mama didn't answer, just stood watching me. Then she shook her head. "Nothing," she murmured. She turned back to Daddy. "Never mind. But you'll bring them then? Lots and lots and lots of ribbons?"

"You could come pick them out yourself," Daddy said.

I held my breath. I had a feeling Daddy was holding his breath, too. Mama refuses to learn to drive a car; and for weeks now, she hasn't left the house. She says she can't walk more than a block in this heat, even though Daddy's general store is just three blocks away.

Now, though, all she said was, "No. You choose. Hair ribbons, wrapping presents ribbons. I don't care! Just lots and lots and lots of ribbons."

"I'll bring you the prettiest ribbons in the shop," Daddy said.

"Oh, goody!" Mama said.

And that was that. All day, I was excited to see what Daddy would bring home because I love pretty things. And when I told my friends, Almay and Vanessa, they were excited, too, because we knew Mama would share with us. Mama shares everything, especially what she calls girl things.

And so, when I heard the door open at six o'clock, I came running down the stairs. Mama was in the living room, and she looked up when Daddy came in. Used to be, late afternoon she'd be sitting playing the piano. Nowadays, she mostly sits and stares out the window.

"Here you are, sweetheart!" Daddy said. He dumped the bag out on the table by Mama's chair.

I hurried over to look at them. There were mounds of them—wide pink satin ribbons; blue ribbons with lace edging on them, the kind you see on underwear; plaid ribbons in reds and blues and yellows. There were narrow ribbons that would be great for my hair, fat ribbons for ponytails. The whole table-top was strewn with ribbons.

"Mama?" I said. "Mama, look! Look at how beautiful these are. Oh, Mama, can I have this one?" I held up a wide pink one, plaid with bits of lace sewn along the edge. It was the prettiest ribbon I think I had ever seen, perfect for my ponytail.

Mama stood up and bent over the table. She looked down at the ribbons. Then she turned to Daddy, and I saw that tears had sprung to her eyes.

"What?" I said. "What, Mama? Don't you like them? Aren't they pretty?"

She didn't answer. She just kept looking at Daddy, tears standing out in her eyes, a red flush rising up her neck.

I could feel myself get quiet inside. "Mama?" I said. "What is it?"

"Go to your room, Missy," she said, her voice all quavery.

"But Mama . . ."

"Go on, Missy," Daddy said softly.

I turned and started out of the room. But I hadn't even gotten to the doorway when Mama suddenly sobbed, "How could you?"

I stopped in my tracks.

"How could you?" she said again. "How could you do this? Ribbons? I asked for bacon and bleach and soap powder! Why ribbons! *Ribbons?*"

I was so startled I couldn't move.

"Missy!" Mama said.

"I'm going," I said. "I'm going."

"No!" Mama said. "Come back here."

I came back to where she stood.

"Missy?" she said. "You won't let him tie these on me, will you?"

I shook my head. "No, Mama."

"Promise?" Mama said.

"Yes, Mama," I said. "But Mama? You asked for ribbons."

"No," Mama said. "I asked for bleach. I distinctly asked for bleach!"

"But Mama," I said. "I remember. This morning? I heard you say . . ."

And then I caught Daddy's eye. He was shaking his head at me gently.

"Yes, Mama," I said, because I didn't know what else to say.

"Now remember," Mama said, and I could see that she was shaking. "You promised." And with one hand, she swept the ribbons off the table and onto the floor.

She turned back to Daddy. And then suddenly, she sat down, her shoulders sagging, her hands clenched together in her lap.

For a long minute, Daddy and I just stood there, not speaking, not moving. Then Daddy bent down and put a hand gently on Mama's shoulder. "Why don't you come up and rest now?" he said quietly. "Please, please come upstairs and rest?"

Mama didn't move. Finally, though, she sighed and stood up, taking the hand that Daddy held out to her. "Dear God," she said softly, "I wish you'd leave me alone. All of them. All of you."

"Who, Mama?" I said. "What did we do?"

Daddy shook his head at me again.

"I should never have married," Mama said. "My mama told me that."

"Mama!" I burst out. "Oh, Mama, don't say that! That's mean. And it's not true. You know it's not true."

"It *is* true," Mama said. "You ask Mimi."

I could feel my jaw trembling, and I blinked back tears.

"It's all right, Missy," Daddy said quietly. "She doesn't mean it."

"Oh, but I do," Mama said. "I really do." She turned to me then. "You know?"

I backed up a little and shook my head. I didn't answer. I didn't know. And, with that odd, blank way she was looking at me—well, I didn't want to know.

$\mathcal{T}wo$

Nobody had supper that night, nobody but me.
And I had it in the kitchen, sitting at the table while Geneva
messed around with putting away food. She grumbled the
entire time about all this wasted food and how hard she had
worked to make supper, but no matter how much I hinted,
and even asked outright, she wouldn't talk about Mama—
not a word. Only once she said, "Your mama is your mama."
Like that explained anything. So I gave up and went upstairs
to my room. There was no sound from Mama and Daddy's
room, so maybe Mama was sleeping.

I got out my shoe box from my closet, my box where I
keep secret things. But even then, I didn't look at it, just
stood staring out the window awhile. It was summer, and
everything was in bloom, the trees heavy with leaves, leaves
coated now with the dust of midsummer, no rain for weeks
and weeks. In the tree outside my window, the leaves were
trembling under the weight of a gawky gray and blue bird
that had come to perch there—a kingfisher, one that usual-

ly lived down by the creek. Everything was silent outside, sleepy in the heat. But from the creek, I could hear bull-frogs' deep, throaty sounds. I could picture their throats pulsing, swelling, as they called out their frog love songs.

Or were those sad songs they were crying? Were they croaking out songs about how crazy their world had become?

What was wrong with Mama? Why the temper tantrum about the ribbons—ribbons she had asked for! And why had she said that thing about how she wished she'd never married? Was it Daddy she didn't want? Or was it me?

I turned away from the window, went over to my bed, and plopped down in the middle of it, sitting there cross-legged. I dumped out all the stuff in my box— my rocks, and my fat little notebooks, and the penny that I had flattened on the railroad tracks, and the pictures of Geneva's twins when they were still porch babies, and the newspaper clip-pings about what happened to them—and my lists. I've always written lists. Like when I was a little kid, and Christmas was coming, and everyone was writing to Santa Claus, I never wrote him a single letter. I just wrote lists of things I wanted, and then I wrote out plans for how I would get those things for myself. I think I knew even then that there was no fantasy person who would do things for you, that mostly you'd have to do things for yourself. I think most people figure that out for themselves one day or another. But there was one thing I couldn't do—couldn't figure out for myself, even back then.

I leaned back against my pillows now, remembering that time. It was the summer after first grade. Mama disappeared that whole summer, and neither Daddy nor Geneva would say where she'd gone. They just said she was away. "Away resting, Missy, so don't worry your head none."

Well, my head was worrying. Why would Mama leave

me, I wondered? Mama and I did everything together. We even had an imaginary friend—Chrysanthemum—that no one else could see. We played together, the three of us, Chrysanthemum and Mama and me, and sometimes my real friends, Almay and Vanessa. We built forts out of sofa pillows—which drove Geneva crazy—and made mud pies in the sand under the swings, even went down in the culverts and creek together. Mama taught me piano, and we made up plays together, plays for Almay and Vanessa and me to put on, while Mama did the music. So I couldn't understand why, if she had to rest, she couldn't rest upstairs in her bedroom so I could see her, maybe even climb up in her bed and rest and nap with her. Sometimes, I'd go up and curl up in her closet, wrapping myself in her robe, sniffing at it, like I used to do with my baby blanket. I even fell asleep there a few times, but thank goodness I always woke up before Geneva came looking for me.

That same summer, Almay, Geneva's daughter who is my best friend, went visiting her other grandma way down in Mississippi almost to the gulf, and then my other best friend, Vanessa, got sent to New Hampshire to be out of the heat. So I was all alone, and spent weeks sitting in the kitchen talking to Geneva, till she got tired of me and chased me away. It was awful lonesome, but I got used to it after a while. Until something worse happened, worse than being lonely: Mimi, Mama's mama, came and took me away to her house in Atlanta to stay for the whole time Mama was gone.

I know this isn't nice to say, but it's just as true as Mama being crazy is true: Mimi is *mean*. She's mean and bossy and stiff-like, as if her whole person got dipped in that starch that Geneva cooks up on washing days. And she thinks she knows everything. That summer I took my favorite blanket with me just like I took it everywhere. On the second day there, Mimi took it and cut it up and threw it away. She said

I was too old to be carrying a blanket around, and it was dirty and disgusting besides. Later I found a little piece of it in the trash under the kitchen sink. I rolled it up and tucked it inside this little shiny pocketbook that Mama once gave me. I carried the pocketbook everywhere that whole summer so Mimi wouldn't find out what was in it and maybe take even that little piece away.

I was so lonely then, not just for Mama and my friends, but for Geneva. Geneva always makes sure to look out for me although, God knows, Geneva has enough on her mind with her own family. Still, she seems to think that working for us, cooking meals and cleaning house and doing our laundry, gives her the right to be a mama to me when my own mama is gone or pays me no mind.

Now, I sat up and went to the window again. Shouldn't there be somebody out there who could help when things got crazy? The nuns say God's mother, the Virgin Mary, will intercede with her Son for us and get us what we want. But that doesn't make sense to me at all. First off, I don't believe it would work because she's His mother—and mothers don't have much say over what their boys do. I know that from my very own observations. Look what happened to Geneva, who wouldn't let her twins sign up to go to war, but they sneaked off to enlist anyway and lied about their age, and both of them got to be sailors. And then both of them got killed, bombed out on their ships. And then, the Virgin Mary couldn't keep her own Son from getting Himself killed. So I don't put a whole lot of stock in her.

So where did that leave me now? Could God—or Mary—help with Mama? Or not?

I thought not. Certainly God doesn't have time. He has this whole messy world on His hands, a big war in Europe, with ships getting sunk; and bombed-out children in England with huge, scared eyes staring out at you from the newspaper every night. So why would He pay attention to little kids praying for a pet rabbit or some chalk for their blackboard or their mama? He wouldn't.

I turned away from the window and went to get ready for bed. I'd find a way to help Mama myself. I didn't know how, but I would. And that way came faster than I ever could have thought.

It was late that night, and I was sound asleep, when suddenly I awoke. It was dark in my room, just a bit of moonlight shining through the window. But something had awakened me. And then I saw—saw Mama sitting on the side of my bed, looking down at me."Mama?" I said.

"Hush," she whispered.

"What's the matter?" I said. I sat up, pulling the sheet with me.

"Shhh!" she whispered. "Nothing's the matter. I was just watching you sleep. You're very beautiful, you know."

I flopped back down in bed and closed my eyes. She woke me up in the middle of the night to tell me that? It wasn't even true. I'm plain as a sparrow.

"You look heavenly when you sleep," Mama said. "So sweet. So beautiful."

"Mama!" I said, turning away from her and tugging the sheet back to my chin. "I'm trying to sleep!"

Mama laughed, a sweet, small giggly sound. "I'm sorry, Missy," she said. "But I just wanted to ask you something. Can you wake up enough for that?"

I waited a minute, then turned back to her slowly and opened my eyes. "I guess," I said.

"Can you keep a secret?" she said.

I was still asleep practically, could hardly clear my head, but my heart had begun to thunder hard and I could feel myself getting tense inside. What secret?

"Do you want to go somewhere with me? Somewhere

secret?" Mama said softly. "Just the two of us?"

I didn't answer.

"Someplace you'll love," she said.

I just looked at her.

"We've been there before," she said. "You loved it. Loved the rooms, the staircases."

I began to be more awake then. Was she talking about the trips that she and Daddy and I had taken, times we've stayed in that beautiful hotel by the water? I loved those times. I loved the water.

"By the water?" I said.

"Exactly," Mama said, smiling at me. "By the water. Just you and me."

"Just you and me, Mama?" I said, fully awake now. I sat up again. "Not Daddy?"

"No. Not Daddy. Just you and me."

"But why?" I said. "I mean . . . ?"

She was quiet a minute, then said softly, "Because I miss my little girl. I know I worried you earlier tonight. I didn't mean to. I guess I was just feeling a bit down and blue." She ran a hand across my forehead, brushing back my hair. "You're growing up so fast," she said. "Motherhood just seems to zoom by. One minute, your little girl is a baby. Next minute, she's almost grown."

I just blinked at her. And then I said, "Oh," because for the life of me I couldn't think of another thing to say. I mean, she had been acting all crazy-like before. And now, well, she sounded fine, normal and sensible and . . . and it was the middle of the night!

"Sound like fun to you?" Mama said. "A little time away?"

"Yes," I said. Because it did.

"Good. But remember, it's a secret. So don't tell."

"Not even Daddy?"

She put a hand on my shoulder, gently pushing me back into my pillow. "No. Not even Daddy. Not yet, anyway. Now, you go back to sleep. We'll talk about it more tomorrow. We'll have a wonderful time; I promise."

She pulled the sheet up under my chin, tucking me in.

As soon as she was gone, I sat up again, grabbed my pillow, and hugged it to me. For about a full minute, I just sat there hugging it, staring at the door. What was happening with Mama now? Was she back to normal, regular again? She hadn't said a word about crazy things, ribbons and bleach and people who wouldn't leave her alone. And if she truly needed just some time with me to make her better, that was fine with me. Yes, she had woken me up in the middle of the night to talk about it. But that wasn't crazy, not for Mama, anyway.

I lay back down. I wasn't sure. But there was one thing I was sure of—it was the middle of the night. And I was too tired to think anymore. I tucked my pillow under my head and turned to face the wall, curled up in a little ball, my knees pulled up the way I like them. Sleep. I would go to sleep. And when I woke up—I'd figure it all out in the morning.

Three

"Bored!" I said. "I'm totally bored. Somebody say something. Do something."

"Hmmm," Vanessa muttered.

"Hot," Almay whispered.

I looked across the porch at my two best friends. It was early the next morning, and Mama was still asleep, her door shut, her blinds closed against the sun. But my friends had been here for hours, Almay swinging in the porch swing, one brown leg tucked up under her, the other gently keeping the swing moving. It was the only breath of air moving at all.

Across from her, Vanessa was lying face down flat on the porch floor, her wild red hair spread out around her. She was trailing her fingers over the edge of the porch, making swirls and circles in the dirt. We'd all been sitting or lying around like this for an hour. It was too hot to move and too boring for anything.

The whole summer had been like this. The sun baked

everything, so that even the grass that got watered overnight, turned all brown by noontime. And the trees wilted, and there weren't even any flowers but the ones that grew up in the culverts, the ones that were really weeds. Locusts and katydids screamed in the trees at nights, warning of the heat that was going to get worse. I always think they're gloating about it: hot, hotter, hotter, they chirped and squawked.

And we had had nothing to do but lie around and be bored—hot and bored. Except now I had that trip with Mama to look forward to. I was dying to say something to my friends, but I had promised Mama. And besides, with Mama, it might never happen, anyway.

"Want to go to Willowware?" I said.

"Too hot," Vanessa said.

"Too mosquito-y," Almay said.

Willowware is what we call our secret place in the side yard under an old cottonwood tree, a place where vines hang down all the way to the ground so thick that no one can see you. We've been going there forever. It's the best place for hiding out and telling secrets and being away from grown-ups. We named it after a plate that Geneva has that she says is special, a willowware plate, she calls it.

"We could bring our lunch," I said.

"The mosquitoes would carry it away," Vanessa said. She scratched at a huge red welt on her shin. "Look at this! Just walking through the grass, I got this."

"OK," I said. "How about this? Let's go to Slow Pond."

"Right, Missy!" Almay said. "And who do you think's going to take us?"

I looked at Vanessa. She was so flat and still on the floor, she could have been a rug. "Vanessa?" I said.

"Hmmm," she said, drowsy-like. "I want to go, sure. But my mama can't take us. She's got bridge today."

"Afterward?" I said.

"Nah," she said. "They stay right till supper time."

We were all quiet for a while. Nobody suggested Almay's mama Geneva, because she works all day—works for us. And of course, since Mama can't drive, no one would suggest her.

"Then let's go alone," I said. "Just us."

Almay looked over at me, her huge brown eyes getting even more huge. "Alone? Slow Pond?" she said. "You crazy, girl? You know we can't go alone."

"Why not?" I said.

"Why not?" Almay said. "Because my mama would kill me, that's why not."

I grinned at her. "Only if she finds out," I said.

I turned to Vanessa. She had struggled up to a sitting position, and she was beginning to smile, her green eyes seeming to sparkle in her little pointed face. "Yeah, Missy," she said. "Let's! Why not? We're all good swimmers."

"Right," I said. Sometimes, I think Vanessa just lives for trouble. Maybe it's why I like her so much. I grinned at her and turned back to Almay.

"Vanessa will," I said. "And I will."

Almay frowned and let out this puffy, exasperated breath. "How?" she said finally.

"What do you mean, how?" I said.

"How would we get there?" she said.

I stood up, tugging at my shorts, pulling them away from my bottom. "Like this," I said, and I began walking across the porch. "See? One foot in front of the other."

"Funny," she said. "But it's two miles, at least! And you know we'll get killed if we get found out."

"So who's going to find out?"

"You know who's going to find out," Almay said. "My mama. You can't keep nothing from her."

"Can, too."

"Sure," she said. "Like we're smart enough?"

I just made a face at her. Geneva is smart, no question about it. But she's not like God, knowing everything, like the nuns say. Though, sometimes I have to admit that it seems that way. Well, she just didn't have to find out, that's all. Right now, she was in the kitchen and the smell of cabbage and onions and bacon was drifting out to the porch.

Vanessa stretched her arms up over her head, then lifted her shirt away from her stomach and waved it, to get some cool breeze. "We've never gone to Slow Pond without a mama or papa to watch for us," she said. "You don't believe that stuff about alligators, do you?"

"Course not," I said. "Though my daddy said he saw one once. But that was out beyond the bend. If you stay in the sandy beach part, it's fine. We've been there zillions of times."

"Yeah," Vanessa said.

"Anyway," I said, "even if a mama was there, what could she do if she saw an alligator?"

"I know what my mama would do," Vanessa said. "Run."

"Mine would wrestle it, probably," Almay said. "But you know she's going to kill us."

"Will you stop it?" I said. "How's she going to find out?"

"The way she always finds out everything. I guess your mama wouldn't go with us?"

"She can't drive," I said. I knew that Almay knew, too. But I also knew Almay said that just to put off saying yes, though I knew that eventually she'd agree. She always goes along with whatever Vanessa and I suggest. It just takes her a while.

"Then let's do it," I said. "We'll meet at the corner in ten minutes. We'll get our bathing suits and towels and . . ."

"And a float," Vanessa said. "I'll bring it. And something to drink."

"I'll bring cookies if I can get them," I said. "If Geneva—
if Almay's mama—leaves the kitchen."

I always feel awkward calling Geneva by her first name
in front of Almay. It seems kind of rude. But Geneva's just
always been Geneva to me, ever since I was a baby.

"We have cherries at home," Almay said. So I knew that
meant she'd go, too.

I grinned at her. "OK! See you," I said.

"See you," Vanessa said, and she leaped down the porch
steps and sped off around the corner of the house, her hair
flying.

Almay got up and went down the steps slowly, dragging
her feet, heading down the lane for her house. "You're
crazy, Missy," she said over her shoulder. "You know that?"

"I know," I said, but I was laughing as I watched her go,
thinking how different she and Vanessa are. It's not just that
their skins are different colors—everything about them is
different. One moves slow, one moves fast; one is daring, the
other timid. And they are both my best friends in the whole
world. And now all three of us were in this together, doing
something we had never done before. I was excited. But if I
was honest, I had to admit that I was a little scared, too—not
of alligators, but scared about getting caught. Almay was
right. Geneva would kill us, and Mama and Daddy would be
real bugged out about it. Still, it was better than sitting
around being bored out of our skins. And anyway, how were
Geneva or Daddy or Mama or anyone else going to find out?
Nobody would see us because nobody goes to the pond this
early in the morning. We'd have the place to ourselves.

I went around the house and in by the front way, not
wanting to meet Geneva in the kitchen and have her ask
questions. Instead, I went up the front stairs and into my
room.

I keep my room super neat, all but for my closet. For

some reason, I love the mess in the closet.

Now I got my bathing suit and goggles and towel from the floor of the closet, got out of my clothes, put on my bathing suit, then put my shorts and shirt on top so no one would notice. The house was quiet, Mama still asleep, Daddy off at the store. I wondered when Mama would get up and tell me more about her plan. But I knew I couldn't ask until she brought it up again. That's how it is with Mama. And besides, by this morning, she might even have forgotten what she had said last night.

I tiptoed down the stairs, then stopped, listening. If Geneva was in the kitchen, there was no way I could get cookies.

But as I stood listening, I heard the sound of sweeping on the front walk, the broom going back and forth, back and forth, quiet and regular-like. I slipped into the kitchen, grabbed a handful of Oreos, and slid them into a paper bag. Then I went out the back way, down the steps, around the other side of the house, and up the alley between us and the Murphys'. And there, on the corner, were Almay and Vanessa already waiting; Vanessa with the float under her arm, Almay with a sack of food and a rolled-up towel. We were off to Slow Pond. And I didn't even care if we met an alligator.

Four

We were so hot we were about melted by the time we got to Slow Pond and couldn't wait to dive into the water. But as soon as we came around the bend of the cove to where the little beach was, we all stopped short and looked at one another. How could we not have realized this? With the heat the way it was, of course people would be here, no matter how early it was! I saw Mrs. Potts from down the street, with her little twin boys, Arthur and James; and Mrs. Jordan who lives across the way, with her two little babies; and a whole bunch of the Henry kids; and Mrs. Montana from our church, with her trio of little girls, each of them about one year apart. And lots of others.

"Uh, oh," I said.

"Told you," Almay said.

We backed up a little to where the live oaks dripped their branches to the ground. For a minute we stood there, hidden by the vines.

"Let's go home," Almay said.

"Not me," I said.

"Just act normal," Vanessa said. "So what if we're here? We're allowed."

"Right," I said. "And we'll put our towels over there, far away from them." I pointed to a little hill of sand at the edge of the beach, where the cove bends around. It's hedged in by weeds and some scraggly bushes. "They'll see us there, but so what? We won't stop and talk or anything. Let them think we're allowed."

"Except we're not," Almay said.

"Will you hush up?" I said. "Let's go." And I walked out onto the beach and up to the little hill, Vanessa following me and Almay trailing after her.

We spread our things out on the little mound of sand. I deliberately didn't look anywhere else, trying—hoping—to be invisible.

"Mrs. Potts is waving at us," Almay said.

"So?" I said. "Wave back."

I turned and waved, and so did Vanessa and Almay.

"See?" I said. "No big deal. They just think we're old enough now to be here without adults so they won't even mention it."

Not that I was too sure of that. But I wasn't going to let it spoil my day, either.

And then I said, "Race you to the water!"

Before I could even finish my words, Vanessa was flying across the sand, her ponytail flipping around behind her, her skinny legs churning up sand and mud.

I raced after her and Almay after me. All three of us dove in, sending up splashes of water circling around us.

I swam out a ways, swimming hard and fast, passing Almay and then Vanessa, letting out all the energy that had been stored up in my arms and legs for weeks—all those weeks of lying around being roasted hot. When I had swum far enough, I flipped over on my back and lay there paddling lightly, looking up at the sky. Sometimes I think I must be part fish, the way I love water. I'm a strong swimmer, lots better than Vanessa or Almay. No one ever taught me, either. I just started coming here with my mama and one day, I must have been about six or so, I was swimming right alongside her. When we got home that day, Mama told Daddy that I was just a natural-born swimmer. I still remember how proud Mama was of me.

Now I lay on my back floating, looking up at the blazing hot white sky, colorless, the way it gets to be in June in Mississippi—no clouds, just hot, white heat. I lay for a long while, not thinking much of anything, just floating and feeling the coolness of the water. After a while, though, I began to think about what Mama had said last night, and I wondered if it would really happen. I loved that hotel, the beach and the water, the waves, the shorebirds. And it was a chance to help Mama get better. But you just couldn't tell with Mama, so I wasn't actually counting on it.

After I had soaked up enough water so I could feel my fingers getting all crinkled up, I turned over and slowly swam back in. Almay and Vanessa were already lying on the sand, side by side, giggling.

When I plopped down beside them, Vanessa turned to me. "Almay's in love," she said.

"So what else is new?" I said.

"Am not!" Almay said. "I just said he's just kind of cute."

"Who this time?" I said.

Almay picked at the mosquito bite on her shin, then looked up at me, smiling, but sort of shy looking. "Jordie," she said.

"Jordie?" I said. "Jordie who? Jordie from the camps?"

Almay nodded.

"*That* Jordie?" I said.

"What's wrong with that?" Almay said, squinting up her eyes at me.

"Nothing," I said. "Except that your mama will kill you."

"She won't find out," Almay said. "And besides, I just talk to him."

"Is he nice?" Vanessa asked. "Remember last summer and him setting fires?"

"That was nothing," Almay said. "He was just trying to kill the rats. He told me all about it."

I remembered last summer, remembered all the things I'd heard about Jordie—and seen for myself, even. He lived in the migrant camps down the lane behind us, behind where Almay lives. His family left in the fall after picking time, but he and his pa came back again this summer. People say Jordie's gotten even bigger—and meaner—than he was last year. Last summer, the police and firemen came because he was setting fires. He coaxed rats out of their holes with food, and then when they came out, he poured gasoline on them and threw a match. People say the rats went running every which way, squeaking and squealing and burning up. Just thinking about it gave me shivers.

"How did you get to meet him?" I asked.

Almay shrugged. "He comes by on his motorcycle," she said. "He promised me a ride some time."

"Isn't he old?" I said.

"Just fourteen," she said. She grinned at me, showing that little gap between her front teeth. She has tiny teeth, but even and white, like little ferret teeth. "Almost my age."

"Your age!" I said.

"What's two years?" Almay said.

"Three years," I said.

She won't be twelve for another six months, come next February. Still, she's got boys on the brain all the time. I swear, she'll have a steady boyfriend before she's out of seventh grade.

"So?" she said. "My papa is older than my mama by seven years! That's nothing!"

I made a face at her.

"The only boy I like is Arthur," Vanessa said.

"Arthur?" I said. "Who's Arthur?"

"Arthur Potts," Vanessa said, nodding her head in the direction of the twins.

I laughed. But I agreed with her. Arthur Potts and his twin brother, James. They're OK—for boys. They're three years old.

"Well, Matthew Winkler, too," Vanessa said.

"Matthew Winkler?" I said. "He looks up girls' skirts."

"Does not!" Vanessa said.

But we all burst out laughing, remembering the school yard last year, and how he always hung around under the jungle gym at recess time and how the girls were always screaming at him.

Suddenly, there was screaming now, shouting, somebody screaming bloody murder. Somebody who sounded terrified.

All three of us jumped to our feet.

"What?" I said, looking around. There at the edge of the water was Mrs. Montana, a baby in her arms, and beside her, Mrs. Potts, holding one little boy by the arm. With her other hand, she was frantically trying to pull off her swimsuit cover-up, yelling, "He can't swim; he can't swim!"

I looked where she was looking. Out in the pond, far out—too far out—arms flailing, head bobbing up and down—a child. A little child.

I looked around me. Nobody was moving. Everyone seemed frozen.

Was it one of the twins?

I didn't wait to find out. I flew down the beach and dove into the water. I swam hard, fast, my legs propelling me, arms thrust out, back, out, back. I kept my head up, eyes on the little head, looking like just a dot in the water now. Behind me, it was silent suddenly, no screaming, maybe because I was too far out to hear.

Hold on, hold on, I'm coming, I said to him inside my head. *I'm coming. I'm coming.*

And then—oh, God—where was he? Had he gone underwater? Or had I just lost sight . . .?

No. No! Please, no.

And then—he was there, bobbing back up to the surface again.

Oh, God, oh, thank you, oh . . . I swam even harder, never taking my eyes off that little dot of a head. I could tell he was sinking lower again, almost gone now, hair floating on top, out and away from him.

Hang on, I'm almost there, I told him. And then I was there. Where he had been. But he was gone. Just sun sparkling on the water. I paused, doggie-paddling. Right there he had gone under. Wait. Watch. He'd bob up again.

He didn't.

Please, God, please.

I waited one more second.

Nothing. Not even a bubble rising.

I took a deep breath. And dove. Down. Down. It was dark, muddy, the water all churned up, mud swirling from the bottom. Good. It meant he was here. Had been here.

I tried to hold still, not churn it any further, just lay underwater, my eyes straining to see. Bits of sunlight filtered through the water. Not enough to see.

Where? Where was he?

Nothing.

One more second, then I resurfaced. I looked around once more in case he had come back up. No. I sucked in air, a huge breath, then dove again. Down, down. There! There was something. On the bottom, mud, and—and something. An arm. I grabbed. Slithery, slippery.

It slipped away.

My lungs were bursting, aching, but I couldn't go back up. I almost had him.

I reached again. Hair. Hair like seaweed. Floating past.

I grabbed it and held on. I kicked my feet, a tremendous burst of energy, no air left. And then I burst out into sunlight above the water, dragging him up behind me. I sucked in air, my breath coming all raggedy, then got an arm around him. A hand under his chin. His head above the water.

I gasped, spit out water, sucked in air, big gulps.

Skinny little kid, limp, dangling, eyes closed, chin in my hand. I doggie-paddled hard, holding him up, keeping myself afloat. Then, I turned him over onto his back and swam toward the beach, one hand cupping his chin, pulling him along behind me.

I got near to shore. Got my feet down. I lifted him in my arms. James. It was little James.

His mom was waist deep in the water, wading toward me, both arms reaching for him. I was gasping for breath, and I let him down into her arms, then waded to shore. I turned and tried to take him back from her, wanted to lay him down and try pumping him out. But she didn't let me, held on tight to him, and it didn't matter, anyway. Because at that moment, he started to cough. And then he started to cry. And then he began to scream. And then he threw up.

For a long while, everyone circled around him, fussed around him and his mom. And then it was like they all noticed me at once. People began hugging me, the mamas and even the little kids. I saw Vanessa and Almay standing there, smiling at me, shy looking.

"Oh, Missy, thank you, bless you!" Mrs. Potts said,

hugging me. "Oh, thank you, bless you, thank you."

She let go of me and turned and hugged her boys, and then she yelled at them, and then she turned to me again, tears just running down her face. "You saved his life!" she said. "Oh, tell your mama; tell your papa. What a wonderful girl you are, Missy. You really are so . . . , oh, I'll tell them myself. Oh, what can I say?"

She was sobbing, and she hugged me again. And then I realized suddenly that I was crying, too. I didn't know why. I just knew tears were running down my face, and I was shivering madly. I had saved his life. I had. But anyone would have done that. It's just that I happened to be there. And I'm a good swimmer.

And then—and then I had a terrible thought. I looked at Almay and Vanessa and they at me. And from the looks on their faces, I knew that all three of us were probably thinking the same thing at the same time: everyone would know. Everyone would be talking about this.

Almay and Vanessa and me—we were in trouble. Big, big trouble.

Five

When we got back into town that day, Vanessa scooted off to her house, and Almay trudged off down the lane, each of us scared to death about what would happen when our parents found out where we had been. Because there was no doubt that they would find out.

And they did find out. In fact, they'd found out before we even got home. The people who had been at Slow Pond told other people, and I guess phones had been ringing all over town. Mrs. Potts's husband, James's daddy, is the doctor for just about everybody in the town, and his nurse told someone and that someone called somebody. Even Geneva had heard before I got home, how I don't know, and she told Mama. Mama called Daddy at the store, but he had already heard. So by the time I got there, Mama and Daddy were already on the side porch, waiting for me. And—who can understand grown-ups—they weren't mad! Not yet, anyway. They just sat down with me and insisted that I tell them everything, the whole thing, every single detail about what had happened. Because, of course, with all the different people telling the story, they already had ten different versions.

So I told them, told them exactly what had happened. Daddy's eyes got wide as I talked. I told about how dark it had been under the water, told about James's arm slipping out of my grip, told about the mud and the fear and not being able to breathe. I realized again in telling it, how scared I had been. I even began trembling as I told it, just as it had happened back at the lake. And Daddy, well, I could almost feel him holding his breath. He kept shaking his head back and forth and back and forth, closing his eyes as if he was picturing it all. He didn't say anything till I was all finished. And then all he said was, "Thank God you were there. Thank God for that."

Did that mean I wasn't going to get into trouble? But I didn't think I should ask that, not yet, anyway.

I turned to Mama. She was sitting next to me on the porch swing, and I could feel her breathing fast and shallow, almost as if she had been running—or swimming with me. She began plucking at her dress, and then at her hair, plucking it so hard around her forehead that I was afraid she'd pull it out.

"It's all right, Mama," I said, taking her hand away from her hair and holding it. "It maybe—well, it wasn't that scary. Maybe I'm exaggerating a bit."

"Oh, my little bird, my dear little bird," she whispered.

I just looked at her. What little bird? Me? Or little James?

"It's all right," I said. "James is all right."

And then, before I could say another word, neighbors started arriving. They must have seen us sitting there on the porch, and so they came—the Murphys from next door, and the Websters and Mrs. Smart and her daughter, Katie, and later even more people. Some of them brought cookies and baked things and flowers. One of them, Mrs. Arnold, even brought a box of pretty little soaps. And they all wanted to hear me tell the story. So I told it all over again, and they all seemed so proud of me.

I wondered, though, when Mama and Daddy would begin to realize they should be mad at me for going without permission. I figured it would happen sooner or later. But for now, it seemed that nobody much cared about me being disobedient.

Well, that wasn't exactly true. Geneva cared. When I went out in the kitchen for a glass of water, she gave me this real big hug and told me that God would bless me for the rest of my days for saving a life. And then she swatted my behind and told me that Almay was grounded for a week, maybe a year, and if my mama was smart, she'd ground me, too. And I should be ashamed of myself for going off without permission.

Well, if I had asked permission, she would have said no. And that might have meant that James would have drowned—right? I didn't think though, that it would be good to say that to her.

Later that night, after supper, Mama and Daddy and I went out to sit on the porch again. The big ceiling fans were making soft whirring sounds above our heads, when Dr. Potts came up the walk. With him was Mr. Montana, the father of the three little girls who had been at the lake. Between them, they carried a huge basket tied up with ribbons.

The two of them came up the steps and placed the basket on the floor of the porch. "For this brave young lady," Dr. Potts said, smiling at Mama and Daddy and then turning to me.

I had stood when they came up on the porch, the way

I'm supposed to do with grown-ups, and Dr. Potts grabbed me and hugged me to him, hard. I was a little embarrassed but then he let go and I was able to bend and look in the basket. It was beautiful, wonderful, packed with all sorts of good stuff. There was fruit and cookies and candies, and on the top was a box of those jelly candies that I love so much, lemon and orange slices covered with sugar.

"Thank you," I said, feeling shy and happy, all at the same time. "It's just beautiful!"

Mama and Daddy waved them into chairs, and they sat, which meant I could sit too. I sat on the porch floor and inched closer to the basket, wondering if it would be polite to dig into it yet. But after a look from Daddy, I put my hands back in my lap.

"There was no need to do that, Jim," Daddy said. "But we do thank you."

"We can't do enough for Missy," Dr. Potts said. "I wish there was more we could do."

"How is the little bird?" Mama asked.

"James?" Dr. Potts said. "He's fine. Tucked in bed, safe and sound." His voice did something funny then, sounding almost like he was going to cry. But when I looked up at him, he was just tugging at his mustache.

"My wife and I have been thinking. And talking," Dr. Potts said. "And we've been talking to Jess and Charlie here."

He nodded his head to the side, and I knew he meant Mr. Montana and his wife.

"We think James and Arthur and all the kids should learn to swim," Dr. Potts went on. "Today we learned just how important it is. And Charlie here made an offer we can't refuse."

"Well, you could refuse it, but you'd be a darn fool!" Mr. Montana said. He burst out laughing.

Mr. Montana is a huge man, not so much fat as just huge. And when he laughs or talks, he laughs and talks huge, too. I always want to put my hands over my ears when he talks.

"Well yes, I did have an idea," Mr. Montana went on, when he was finished laughing. "We're almost finished putting in our new swimming pool. Too hot for the ladies to be going all the way to that lake. Yes. So we'd like to suggest something."

He turned to me. "How would you like to earn some money this summer?" he said. "How would you like to teach the little ones to swim?"

"Me?" I said.

He nodded.

"In your pool?" I said.

He nodded again.

"Oh, wow!" I said. A swimming pool! In this heat. And just down the street! No more being bored. No more Almay and Vanessa and me hanging around looking for something to do. We could play in the pool. And I'm good with little kids. Really good.

"That's most kind of you," Daddy said, before I was able to even speak because of the thoughts running around in my head like little mice. "But I don't think you should pay her. I'm sure Missy would be glad to do it just to help out."

"Oh, I would!" I said. Even though that wasn't completely true. But if I could play in a swimming pool every day—I'd almost pay *them*!

"No," Dr. Potts said. "We'd insist. We've been over this and we insist. So what do you think, Missy?"

"My friends, too?" I said.

Dr. Potts looked at Mr. Montana.

"I don't see why not," Mr. Montana said. "We have five little ones all together. Another set of hands would be real helpful."

"Two other sets of hands," I said.

"Two?" Mr. Montana said.

"Yes. You know," I said. "Vanessa and Almay."

"Oh!" he said. He looked at Dr. Potts.

Dr. Potts wasn't looking back.

"Almay is Geneva's daughter, right?" Mr. Montana asked slowly, turning back to me.

"Yes, sir," I said. And I began to feel nervous. Because I suddenly had a feeling that I knew maybe what he was thinking, the same thing Geneva is always saying to me: *I'm my color and you're your color, and don't you forget it.*

Mr. Montana looked up at Mama and Daddy. I turned to them, too. It had gotten almost completely dark on the porch, and I couldn't see their faces at all, couldn't see if they were looking back at him or what their looks said. Daddy was tipped back in his rocker, and Mama was far back in the corner on the swing. All I could see were the tips of her white shoes, gently pushing the swing back and forth. Nobody spoke, but I could hear Mama humming in that tuneless way she has of doing sometimes, no song, just a little sound like a motor running softly.

"Well," Mr. Montana said, after a while. "Yes. Um, well. I don't think . . . I don't think Almay would want to do that now, would he?"

"Oh, she would!" I said. "I know she would."

"Missy," Dad said. "Why don't you go inside and get ready for bed now? You've had a long day."

"But Daddy, I want to . . ."

"Missy!" Daddy said. "Go on, now." There was a warning sound in his voice.

I stood up slowly, feeling myself getting a hot, angry feeling.

"Off you go," Mama said. She tipped forward in the swing to take my hand. "Nighty-night, little bird."

"Night," I said. I took a deep breath. Then I turned and nodded to the others. "Good night," I said.

"Night!" they all called out. Cheerfully. Too cheerfully.

I went into the house, my heart racing, my mind tumbling around. I wouldn't go to their old pool without Almay. I wouldn't. And I wouldn't even tell her that they had offered to let me come—and to pay me besides. Because then I'd have to tell her that they didn't want her. I knew why. Because she was a different color. And her mama was a maid. And my own mama and daddy hadn't spoken up and said a word for her.

But I wanted to go to the pool! I wanted so much to play, to swim!

Well, I wouldn't. I would not do it.

For all I cared, they could all drown.

$S i x$

Next morning I was up early. I had hardly slept, maybe from all the excitement, maybe because I was so mad and confused about the swimming-pool thing. Or maybe because it was so hot in my room. I had flipped my pillow about a thousand times, trying to find a cool spot, and had finally ended up standing by the window half the night, hoping to get even a hint of a breeze.

I was dying to hear what Mama and Daddy had decided. If they said I had to go to the pool without Almay, I was going to tell them no. At least, I thought I'd tell them no. It was already so hot, the temperature probably ninety—and it was just seven o'clock in the morning. Why did it have to be this way? It just wasn't fair.

I could hear Mama and Daddy stirring in their room, then heard the back door open as Geneva came in to begin her day. I wondered if Geneva had overheard anything last night. I hoped not, because her feelings would be hurt. But knowing Geneva, she probably had. And maybe she could tell me something.

I dressed quickly, then slipped down the back stairs and into the kitchen. The minute I came in, Geneva gave me one of her dirty looks, just as she had yesterday. It was obvious she had been chewing things around in her head because she burst out, "Suppose you had been the one who drowned? Then how do you think your mama and daddy would feel? And they'd blame me for not watching out for you."

I didn't answer, just shrugged, then sat down on the old green painted chair by the table. "Geneva?" I said.

"Don't 'Geneva' me!" she said. "Just answer me. And get some sense into your head for a change. Suppose you'd been the one who drowned?"

Which of course made not a bit of sense, since I was the one who could swim. But I also knew that there was no sense arguing with her. Never is. Except then something came over me—something mischievous maybe. Or maybe it wasn't mischievous. Maybe it was real.

"Would you miss me?" I asked, looking up at her.

"What?" she said. "What you say?"

"I said, would you miss me if I drowned?"

She glared at me. "Miss you!" she muttered. "Miss you? You make no sense, no sense at all. Now get on out a my kitchen so I can get my day started."

She waved her hands at me, like she was shooing away a fly or something.

I sighed and stood up. It was clear she was still mad. And when she's mad, she won't talk. "OK," I said. "I'm going."

She didn't even answer.

I started out of the room. I had just gotten to the door when she called out, "Come back here!"

I turned.

She had put on her apron and was tying it up around her back. She didn't look at me, just finished with her apron, then went to the door where she keeps her house slippers. She tugged off her shoes, making grunting sounds as she bent over, then slid her feet into her slippers.

That done, she came to the stove, paying me no mind, as though she hadn't called me back. She began making coffee, taking her time doing it too, carefully measuring out the coffee beans, then grinding them, pouring the water and setting the pot on the stove. She went to the refrigerator and got out eggs and milk and brought them to the table. She opened a drawer, got out some utensils, and went to the cabinet for a bowl, cracking eggs into it.

And all this while she didn't say anything. Not a single word. It was only after she had the eggs in the bowl and was beating them with a little whisk thing that she spoke. But she didn't look up at me.

"I'd miss you," she said. "Now get your sorry self out a here. And don't get a swelled head over what you done yesterday."

I waited just another minute, but she didn't add anything, didn't look at me, either. So I turned and went out on the porch. I hadn't gotten any information, but I knew there was no sense asking for more right now. She was still mad at me, and she'd talk of nothing else till she had it out of her system. And no sense poking at her, either. It only made her more stubborn.

Still I felt a little singing feeling in my heart: she'd miss me.

I settled myself on the porch swing, waiting for breakfast. I sighed, wondering what to do with myself for the rest of the day. Vanessa had called last night, whispering, to say that she was grounded for a week, and then she'd hung up real quick, because she wasn't even supposed to be using the phone. And of course, I already knew about Almay being grounded.

I wondered if I should ask Mama about the trip she had

talked about the other night. But I knew it wouldn't be good to ask. One thing I was surely going to ask, though: what about the pool? What had happened after they sent me upstairs?

After a little bit, I heard Mama and Daddy come downstairs, and I went into the house and we all settled at the dining-room table for breakfast.

As soon as the food was on the table, and Geneva had gone back to the kitchen, I said, "Daddy? Mama? What about the pool? What about the swimming lessons?"

For a minute, neither of them answered. Finally, Daddy said, "What about it?"

"You know," I said.

Daddy looked at Mama. She was looking back, but her face was completely blank, so if Daddy was looking for some signal there, he sure wasn't going to get it.

He looked away. "I don't know, Missy," he said.

He opened his newspaper, and picked up his coffee cup. It's kind of a rule that you don't say much to Daddy before his coffee, and I realized I should have waited. But I couldn't seem to help myself.

"Daddy?" I said.

"Missy, I told you I don't know," Daddy said. "We have to give it some thought."

"Give *what* some thought?" I said.

Daddy just shook out his newspaper and didn't answer.

I looked over at Mama, but she was just sugaring her tea and acted as though she hadn't heard a word.

I made this little growling sound under my breath, and Daddy looked up at me.

I tried to look innocent, but I knew Daddy had heard.

"I want you to stay close to home today," he said. "I don't want any more of the shenanigans we had yesterday."

I sighed. I had known this would happen, that they'd

begin to realize they were mad at me for going off without permission. "I guess I'll go to the library," I said.

I had meant it to sound virtuous, good, but it came out surly sounding.

"Well, make sure you tell someone where you're going. Me or your mother or Geneva."

"I always tell!" I said.

Daddy's eyebrows went up.

I shrugged.

"And don't be flip about it," Daddy said.

I took a deep breath. "Yes, Daddy," I said.

I looked across the table at Mama again.

She was watching Daddy and me, looking from one of us to the other. When she saw me looking at her, she smiled, then looked down at her hands in her lap.

We all went about eating breakfast, nobody saying much. But I was thinking and thinking. I thought about the pool—about swimming lessons—about Almay. What did Daddy have to "think about?" Had Mr. Montana said yes or no? And what had Daddy said? Why couldn't he just tell me?

After a while, Daddy folded his newspaper, wiped his mouth with a napkin, then stood up, came round the table, and kissed Mama on the top of the head. "Enjoy your day, sweetheart," he said. "Try to stay cool."

" 'Bye, James," Mama said.

Then Daddy came round the table to me. He kissed the top of my head, too. "You're a good girl," he said softly.

I just looked up at him. A *good girl*? Me? When he'd just been scolding me?

Who could understand grown-ups? But I was glad that he'd said it, glad that he wasn't mad. " 'Bye, Daddy," I said.

And then he was gone.

The minute he was out the front door, Mama leaned

across the table. "How would you like to take our trip today?" she asked quietly.

"What?" I said.

She just smiled.

"You mean to the beach?" I said. "That place? The hotel place?"

Mama nodded again. So she hadn't forgotten!

"Just us?" I said.

"Just us."

"Does Daddy know?"

"Not yet."

"But you're going to tell him?"

Mama nodded.

I looked at her for a minute, and she looked back, eyebrows up, a kind of soft look on her face, a little smile playing around her mouth. I smiled back at her, not wanting her to know I was studying her, even though I was. She seemed all right. Normal. Not too up, not too down. Just excited and happy.

I took a deep breath. Well, I was excited, too. "Good!" I said.

"Hush!" Mama said. "I don't want Geneva to know."

"Why not?"

"Just because. You'll see. Now go upstairs and get packed. But remember, nobody is to know. Don't let Geneva see you packing. Just put in some pretty things. We'll have dinner in that nice dining room, remember it? And take a sweater. It gets chilly at night."

I jumped up from the table.

"Don't forget your swimsuit," Mama said. "You can swim all you want in the gulf. Who cares about a measly little swimming pool?"

Well, I did. But I wasn't going to talk about that right now. Right now, I had bigger things to think about.

Seven

And that's how come we ended up on a bus in the middle of the day, when Daddy was off to work and Geneva had gone to the grocery store. And in just a few hours, Mama had us settled in this fancy hotel on the coast, where we could see the water right from the porch.

This was the hotel I had come to with Mama and Daddy a few times before, and I loved it, loved the water, loved the fancy dining room. There was even a pool, though I liked swimming in the gulf the best.

It was fun being in this splendid place that day, just the two of us off on a holiday. We had a wonderful dinner in the dining room—I ordered shrimp, my favorite— and then we sat out on the porch when it got dark, just talking and enjoying the coolness of the sea breeze. For a long while we sat there, watching fireflies light up here and there under the branches. Mama made up a sweet poem about them, about how their little lamps guided the stars at night. And then when we were both tired out, we went on up to bed. Mama seemed so good, so rested and peaceful that—even though I didn't like the idea of her not telling Daddy where we were—I could tell it was good for her to be here.

But next day, we didn't go back home. We stayed another day. And then another. And another. And all that time, Mama wouldn't call and tell Daddy where we were. She was so excited those days, happy and chattering all the time, even laughing and flirting with the waiters in the dining room. But whenever I mentioned home, she got real quiet.

"Your daddy will find out," she said. "All in good time."

"But Mama?" I said on the third day. "Somebody should know. If you don't want to call, could I do it? Can I just call Geneva and let her know we're all right?"

"And then she'll tell your father, so no," Mama said. "Or she'll tell Mimi. We don't want that to happen, do we?"

There was something sad in Mama's eyes when she said that.

"All right, Mama," I said quietly.

Mama stood up and hugged me then. "This is our secret time together, just you and me," she said. She swung me around. "It's our time to drift and sing and float on a breeze! Right, my little bird?"And that was the last thing she said about it. Of course, I was tempted to use the phone and call myself. But I was never in the room with the phone unless Mama was there, too. And anyway, maybe Mama was right—maybe just a quiet rest in this place would make her better again. Maybe being with me could make her better again too.

Except she wasn't getting better. Every single time we left the room and then came back, Mama went about opening and closing every single dresser drawer and peeking inside. She even took a drawer out and dumped it over once, checking the underside. She said that was something women had to think about when traveling alone—that someone could be hiding in our rooms.

"In a *dresser drawer*, Mama?" I asked.

"Oh, yes," Mama said. "That's happened to me more than once."

I looked at her to see if she was joking, but she wasn't. She just went on checking everywhere—even inside her hat-box!

But the worst thing that happened was that even though she had promised, she wouldn't let me go to the beach or even in the pool. All she would say when I begged—and I begged all the time—was, "You may go in to swim, but you may not go near the water." And then she'd giggle. After a while, I stopped fussing about that, because I thought maybe it would be better if I stayed and kept watch over her.

And yet, the funny thing was that at other times, she seemed normal and happy, smiling and nodding and chatting with everyone. And she certainly flirted with all the men. Every night when we sat down in the dining room, with the lamplight shining on us, the men looked Mama over. They do that everywhere she goes. I could see it in their eyes: A beautiful woman, they were thinking. And she is beautiful. But I wondered if any of them could see the muddle that must have been inside her head. I also wondered if it would be right for me to ask the desk clerk if I could use the hotel desk phone and call Daddy? Or not?

I wasn't sure. So I did nothing, and the days stretched out to a week—a whole week!—and I began to worry about other things. Like money. Because it was pretty clear that Mama didn't have any. She couldn't even buy a newspaper, would just pick up ones left on the lounge chairs on the porch. And every time a chambermaid or bellboy did something for us, they'd stand around, not exactly with their hands out, but shifting from foot to foot, waiting for their tips, you could see—well, Mama had nothing for them. Also, we never ate anywhere but the hotel—not even on the boardwalk for an ice cream cone, though I begged. But Mama just said, "We'll eat at the hotel, and that's that."

Finally, one day at the end of the week, I heard the man at the desk ask Mama if she would settle up the bill for the week. Mama got that look on her face that always makes me think of the queen in *Alice in Wonderland*, and very haughty-like, she said, "We'll pay when we check out, thank you very much. I thought I made that quite clear. You know who I am, don't you?"

His ears turned red, and he said, "Right, ma'am, right, of course I know and I didn't mean to trouble you."

Mama gave him one of those long, slow looks she's so good at, and then turned away. But her face was flushed, too, and I know his question had made her a little nervous. And me, well, I could have told the man this much: that bill would not get paid. Not by Mama.

And Mama must have been thinking about it, too. Because it was the very next morning that Mama woke me early. "Missy!" she whispered. "Get up and get dressed. But be quiet."

I looked around. It was still dark outside, just a pale light seeping in around the edges of the window. "Mama!" I said, sitting up in bed. "What time is it?"

"Early," Mama said, with a low laugh. "And it's time to go home. We'll just go quietly, like ladies should."

"But can't we wait till it's light? I'm tired."

Mama just giggled and raised her shoulders. "Why wait? We'll just tiptoe downstairs and outside and catch the bus."

Tiptoe?

"Mama, what are you thinking?" I said. Because even though I was still practically asleep, I was beginning to get a bad feeling that I knew what she was thinking.

"I'm thinking we should just sort of tiptoe away. No need to make a fuss about it."

"You mean we're going without paying, right?" I said.

Mama smiled and gave me that silly shrug of her shoulders, like she does sometimes.

"You can't do that, Mama!" I said.

"Oh?" Mama said. "You just watch me, Missy. You just watch me."

"But what if we get caught?" I said.

"Who's going to catch us?"

"I don't know who! Somebody," I said. "The desk person. The night watchman. He'll call the police."

"Shows what you know," Mama said. "They all adore me." She came to the bed, leaned over me, and hugged me to her. "And I adore *you*," she whispered. "Now get dressed and hurry. And do be quiet."

I looked around the room and saw she had the bags ready, her makeup bottles already missing from the little table, her hatbox all packed. I saw, too, that she was all dressed, makeup and all, so I knew she'd been up a long time and had planned this all out. "Mama," I said, trying one last time. "It's not honest."

"Honest?" Mama said, making a clicking sound with her tongue. "And what about you, Missy? You've been eating the food, too, and staying in the fancy hotel. It didn't seem to bother you, putting all this on the bill."

"But I thought you'd pay!" I said.

"With what?" she said.

Well! How could I answer that?

So, even though I knew what we were doing something wrong, I also knew there was little point in arguing with her. I got dressed, packed my few things, and we went out into the hall, closing the door softly behind us. We didn't take the elevator, just went along the hall, opened the door to the service stairs, and tiptoed down to the street floor. There, Mama put down her bag and tried the door.

Locked. It was locked tight. And even though Mama threw her hip against it, nothing happened. She tried it again, then motioned with her head for me to try it.

I hit it so hard with my hip, I swear I turned all black and blue in an instant.

Mama just looked at me and shrugged. And then she took a deep breath, picked up her bag, drew herself up tall, turned around, and walked out into the hotel lobby. She walked straight through, nodding smartly at the desk manager, and headed for the door, me trailing behind, hoping to be invisible, my heart pounding in my chest, my throat so dry I could hardly swallow.

"Ma'am!" the desk person called.

Mama didn't turn, just waved her free hand, the one that wasn't holding her hatbox and bag, and kept right on going, me practically running to keep up with her.

But before we could get out the door, bells began ringing, and two men in hotel uniforms showed up, one of them really, really huge, and he took Mama by the arm—very gently, though. And he led us back to the desk

And then did the fur fly! The night manager called the day manager, and he came and called more security people, and I think he would have called the police, but Mama put up her hand, just like that *Alice in Wonderland* queen, and she ordered him to give her the phone. Then she called Daddy.

"James," she said. "We're at the Magnolia Hotel. Bring your checkbook and come get us and come quickly because I'm out of clean clothes."

There was some more back and forth, and the night manager had to talk to Daddy on the phone, and then the day manager, and it seemed to be settled.

That over with, Mama took me by the hand, led me to a corner of the lounge, and sat me down beside her. She ordered breakfast brought to us, fresh-squeezed orange juice, and hotcakes, and sausages, and croissants, and oatmeal, and black coffee for her, and hot chocolate for me. I really didn't feel hungry at all, with my heart thumping away like crazy and my stomach jumping around like those Mexican jumping beans you can buy at beachfront stores. But Mama had her mind set on an elegant breakfast and, don't you know, they brought it to us—all that food, plus little tiny jam jars and sweet butter, all spread out on a white tablecloth, with one yellow tea rose in a crystal vase, on a little table that they rolled out just for us, in a corner of the lounge. All this, even though we had tried to sneak out without paying up.

Mama smiled at everyone who came by. Me, though, I just prayed. Prayed that God would make all of this right. Prayed that He'd make all this craziness go away. Prayed most of all that Daddy would get here soon.

Because I couldn't wait to be home. Home meant Geneva and Almay and Vanessa. And Geneva more than anyone could make sense of what had gone on. And even if she couldn't, it would be good to just be with her, to be sitting in that kitchen, watching her snap beans or do whatever it was she was doing. Because Geneva was for sure the most sensible one in my life right then.

Eight

It took a long time, but finally Daddy appeared, angry looking, but scared looking, too—or maybe just worried. He paid the bill and huddled with the managers, and then we started on home, none of us speaking.

After a while, Daddy turned to Mama. "If you wanted a vacation, I would have taken you," he said quietly. "You know that, don't you?"

"I know," Mama said.

"Then why didn't you ask? Say something?"

Mama didn't answer.

"Why didn't you call?" Daddy said.

"I did call," Mama said. "This morning."

Daddy just shook his head.

After a minute, he turned around to me and said, "Why didn't you call, Missy?"

I wanted to tell him the truth—that Mama wouldn't let me. But I didn't want to get her into more trouble with him. So I just shrugged.

He kept on looking at me over the seat, and I wanted to say, please watch the road, but I just kept my mouth shut because I figured I was in even more trouble than Mama. I mean, everyone knew Mama was different. But me, I was supposed to know better. Anyway, believe you me, I was watching the road myself, not wanting to get ourselves killed.

After a moment, Daddy stopped looking at me and he settled into driving. He said that he couldn't figure out why the hotel people hadn't called the police. Well, he wasn't asking me, but I could have told him. It's because Mama is so pretty and has these ways, those looks she gives, that smile that seems to send men off their heads. And when Mama is normal, not crazy-like, she sends everyone off their heads, is so sweet you just want to eat her up. She's that way to me, too.

Used to be, I'd practice her looks by myself in the mirror, to see if I could have the same effect on people. One day, Almay and Vanessa and I all practiced and we tried them on each other. Almay tried this sulky, pouting look of Mama's, with her lip thrust out. But I told her she looked exactly like she was about to throw up. And when I tried on Mama's haughty look, Almay said I looked like I had just smelled dog poop. And Vanessa, she couldn't manage even one look without bursting out laughing.

Anyway, I thought about all those things as the miles went by, looking out the window for some familiar sight that would tell me we were almost home. And then we were. And I can't ever remember being so happy to see my very own house.

As soon as we got inside, Mama went upstairs, saying she wanted to rest, and Daddy went upstairs with her. I wondered what they were saying to each other, now that I wasn't there to overhear. But whatever it was, it couldn't have been much, because after about two minutes, Daddy came down-stairs and went off to the store. And I went right to the kitchen to find Geneva. Almay wasn't anywhere around, and I figured she hadn't come with her mama because maybe she had given up on me and Mama ever coming back.

I set myself on the green painted chair by the table, kicking my foot against the table leg, waiting for Geneva to notice me. She takes her time about that sometimes, espe-cially when something's bothering her. And there's no sense talking or asking her anything while you're waiting, because she just gets stone-deaf. You have to wait till she's good and ready. That's why I was kicking the table. I figured it would get on her nerves eventually, and she'd say something—even if it was, *you quit that!*

I waited a long time, watching her shell lima beans into the chipped, porcelain colander held between her knees. Geneva is as strong and big as a man. Her skin is so black it's almost blue and shiny, too. It's so shiny that at times, when I look at her real hard, I think I can see myself reflected in her skin, see me looking right back at myself. Her eyes are dark, too, black-brown, with squint lines all around the edges. When she smiles—not often—her eyes almost disappear into the folds around them. Her hair is always tied up in a bun in back, but on wash days, when the washing is finished, then she lets her hair down and washes that, too, letting it hang all rich and curly down her back. The shoulders of her dress get all wet with the hair lying there, and once, when I was little, I got a towel and put it on her shoulders under her hair to keep her dress dry. I remember how surprised she looked, and then her eyes got shiny and she put a hand on my head before she turned away. I thought that maybe I had done something wrong, so I never did it again. But I think now that maybe it was something else that made her look that way.

Anyway, I waited now about an hour, or at least it felt like an hour, and finally she spoke to me. "Your mama can't help it," she said. "Something's got ahold of her."

"What kind of something?" I said.

Geneva lifted her huge shoulders, then dropped them, breathing out a sigh at the same time. "She'll let us know when she can, I guess," she said.

"I think she hates Daddy," I said.

"Now where'd you get that foolishness?" Geneva said, squinting up her eyes at me.

"It's not foolishness," I said. "She said one time that she wished she'd never married him. And she left without telling him. Sounds to me like she doesn't like him."

"Sounds like nothing of the sort," Geneva said. "Sounds to me like she's married, is all. Not one thing more than that. That's just how it gets sometimes, after you been married awhile."

Geneva went to the sink, her house slippers slapping against the linoleum, and put the beans under running water. It was quiet in the kitchen, but for the sound of running water.

"Geneva?" I said. "You know what else she said?"

"Never mind what else she said," Geneva answered. "Your mama likes to talk big. And don't you say that again, about her hating your daddy."

"But something's wrong, isn't it?"

"Maybe," Geneva said quietly. "Maybe not. But if there is, we got to give her time to work it out herself. She will. She's no dummy. We've seen times like this before."

"Will she have to go away again?" I said.

Geneva didn't answer.

"Will she, Geneva?" I said. "I won't have to go to Mimi's, will I?"

"God knows," she said. "Only God. He writes the book.

We just bide our time and wait to read it."

"But I won't have to go to Mimi's?" I said again.

I knew it was selfish to think this way. I should have been thinking more about Mama. I had even been praying for her. A lot. Because if God writes the book, like Geneva is always saying, I wanted to be sure He got some information from me first. Still, for the last few days, the thought of going to Mimi's had been haunting me.

Geneva just tightened her mouth and turned away.

I know Geneva doesn't like Mimi any more than I do, though she's never said a word. But when Mimi comes to visit, for a whole week every year at Thanksgiving, Geneva barely budges out of the kitchen. She turns all surly and silent, too, and if I go in the kitchen, she shoos me out. For the whole time that Mimi is here, the house seems upset and out of sorts. I know one reason: Mimi thinks it's wrong for me to be with Geneva so much, and Geneva knows Mimi thinks that. And last Thanksgiving, I also heard Mimi tell Mama that I was too old to be playing with Almay, but Mama just ignored her.

Now Geneva kept rinsing and washing those beans like they were the dirtiest beans that had ever come out of a garden. Then, without turning to me, she said, "You know about having babies, right?"

I sighed and rolled my eyes—and a good thing her back was turned or I might have gotten slapped good for it.

"I know how they get made, if that's what you're asking," I said, trying to sound matter-of-fact.

"And you know about when women get to an age when they don't have no more babies?" she said.

"Yeah," I said. *And don't tell me more because I don't want to know.*

"Well," Geneva said. "I just suspect your mama is at that stage where she's not making babies anymore, and it has her down."

"Why?" I said. "She hasn't had a baby in twelve years. Not since me."

"Still," Geneva said. "It's a stage she's going through, I suspect. And sometimes, it makes women do mighty strange things. Specially if it comes early, like it seems to be doing with your mama."

I figured she meant that change-of-life stuff, but I sure didn't want her talking to me about it. Anyway, I didn't think that was what was wrong with Mama. Why would she want more babies? I mean, that time she said she wished she hadn't married, made it seem like she didn't even want me.

"Just be patient with her, is all," Geneva said, turning to me. "It will pass."

"What if she's crazy?" I said.

Geneva cut her eyes at me. "Just hush with that smart mouth," she said.

"I'm not smart mouthing!" I said. "I'm serious. Do you think she is?"

"No!" Geneva said, turning back to the sink. "I don't. And you just stop thinking it, too, 'cause she ain't crazy. Now, you run on and read your books and get outa my kitchen. I got enough work to do without you sitting here chattering away all the day long."

I got up, but I didn't leave. Tears had come crowding up to my eyes, and I suddenly felt all jerky and trembly, like my insides were fluttering around. It's a feeling that comes over me sometimes, and I never know exactly when it will happen, or even what makes it happen. I just begin to shake all over, my jaw trembling so hard sometimes that I have to clamp my mouth tight shut. When I was little and that happened, the summer Mama went away, Geneva would pull me into her lap and hold me tight against her till the shaking stopped. But later that summer, when I went to Mimi's,

Mimi scolded me bad when she saw me shaking and said to stop being a little misfit. So I learned to just clamp my jaw hard, and if the shaking got too bad, I'd go to my room and wrap myself tight in a blanket and sit on the floor in the closet, my back pressed hard against the wall. And that helped a little.

Now I went to the sink and stood beside Geneva. I looked at her rough old hands, still sifting through the lima beans. I put my hand in the colander alongside hers—didn't take her hand, just let mine be there beside hers, maybe touching just a little bit. For a long time, we stood there that way, not talking, the water just washing over the beans and our hands, while I waited for the shaky feelings to subside.

After a while, Geneva said, "You done good staying by your mama's side all them days."

I looked at her, surprised.

She nodded. "Real good," she said. "I think you should go find your friends now."

I kept on staring at her, but she wasn't looking back. *I was good to stay with Mama?* I thought everybody would be mad at me.

"Almay's been missing you something bad," Geneva went on. "Go on down the lane and find her."

I could go down the lane? Geneva never lets me go down the lane to her house. I always have to wait for Almay to come here. When I asked how come—used to ask, when I was little—Geneva just said that I'm my color and she's her color and that's all there is to it. Which made no sense to me, especially because Almay could come here.

For a moment, I just stood there looking at her, too surprised even to move.

"Well?" she said. "Do you want to go or not?"

"I do!" I said. And I grabbed a towel, wiped my hands

dry, and started for the back door.

"And don't you talk no swimming-pool nonsense, the two of you. You hear?"

"Swimming pool?" I stopped and turned to her. "What about the swimming pool?"

"You heard me," she said, and she waved her hand at me. "Now, go! Get!"

And I did. I was out of that kitchen and out of the house. And running as fast as my legs would take me to find Almay and Vanessa, too. And to find out about the swimming pool, no matter what Geneva said.

Nine

Almay and Geneva live down the lane in back, in a row of old houses. Most of the houses are sort of lop-sided, leaning toward the earth, and the paint is mostly gone from them. Still, they have a nice gray, silvery look, especial-ly at night. The people who live there are Negroes like Almay and Geneva, and they don't like white people mess-ing in their lane. No one especially told me that, but I know; and of course, I know for a fact that Geneva doesn't want me at her house. Still, sometimes, late at night, I go back there and lean in close by Geneva's fence where there's a big old bush that sort of hides me, and I listen and watch. I see people out on their porches, or playing in the dusty road, yelling and laughing and fussing at one another. And there's music. All over the place, music. Almay has the prettiest voice you ever did hear, and sometimes there's singing and even dancing. You most always hear the mamas scolding the yard babies, and someone chasing the porch babies, and there's always someone minding someone else's business.

Sometimes there're fights—I don't mean like with fists, but just fights with yelling. And all the time, there're the big boys strutting around showing off to their girls, and the girls are strutting for the boys, and sometimes you hear just howls of laughing. And dogs! There are dogs everywhere.

I guess maybe it's not nice to spy like that, but I can't help it. I just love watching, because even when they're acting mad, they're strong and good together. At least, it seems that way to me. Anyway, those are the things I was thinking as I ran, feeling free as a bird, away from Mama, away from that hotel, away from all the crazy feelings and worries.

And then, when I got to Almay's house—there she was, she and Vanessa, too—and Vanessa never goes down the lane, either! The two of them were perched on the porch railing, one leaning against one corner post, the other against the other post.

"Missy!" they yelled when they saw me, both of them at the exact same time.

"Where were you?" Vanessa said.

"What happened?" Almay said. "Me and my mama was half-crazy with worrying about y'all."

I came up the steps and sat down on the porch floor, scooting back against the house into the shade, out of the glaring sunlight.

"We were at a hotel," I said.

"A hotel?" Almay said. "What hotel? What for?"

"Was it because your mama was mad at us?" Vanessa said. "That's all I could think about—us going to Slow Pond, and maybe your mama was real mad at us and so she took you away from us."

"No!" I said. "It wasn't that. It was . . . ."

"*Stupid!*" Almay said. "You made my mama half-crazy with worry. She looked for your mama everywhere. Looked for you, too." Almay frowned fiercely at me, mad and mean looking, just like her mama gets when she's worried.

I sighed. I had known that Geneva would be worried, but I had forgotten about the hiding part. What happens is, sometimes when Mama has a bad spell, she goes off into strange places—the attic or closets or such, and Geneva and Daddy and I have to go looking for her. Then, when we find her, we just pretend that we knew she was playing hide-and-seek with us. Geneva then settles Mama into her bed for a nap and watches over her till she's asleep. Sometimes, that works, and when Mama wakes up, she's normal again. And she has no memory of ever having hidden. Or at least, she pretends not to remember.

Now it hurt to think that Geneva had been looking everywhere, worrying and fretting the way I know she does.

"Why didn't you call?" Almay said.

"Because," I said. I took a deep breath. And then I told about where we went and how Mama wouldn't let me call and tell anyone, that she wanted this to be our own secret time together. But I tried to make it sound normal—or sort of normal. Like this was just something that Mama wanted, some time alone with me, that she had wanted it for a long time, and that it didn't have anything to do with our going to Slow Pond—which I was pretty sure it didn't. I even said how sweet Mama had been acting, even though inside my head I was remembering other things. It's not that Almay and Vanessa don't know about Mama being different. It was just that I had had enough of crazy for a whole week. I wanted not to have to think about all that.

"Wow!" Vanessa said, when I was finished. "Was it fun? Was it fancy?"

"Yeah. Fancy," I said. "But boring, too."

"Like the movies?" Almay asked. "Flowers everywhere and silver and chandeliers and all?"

"Sort of. But not really like the movies," I said, remembering the scene this morning with Mama trying to sneak out.

"But why didn't you call?" Almay said again—like a dog with a bone, just like her mama—won't let go of a question until she gets an answer. "Or why didn't *she* call?"

"I couldn't call because she wouldn't let me," I said. "And I don't know about her. Now, come on. Let's do something."

"First Almay has to tell you about Jordie," Vanessa said. She turned to Almay. "Show Missy what happened."

Almay bent and pulled up the lower part of the long, flowy pants she was wearing, showing her curved brown leg—and I swear, I don't know how come her legs are so soft and rounded, when I still have legs like sticks. Just above her ankle, on her inside calf, was a hot-looking, brownish-red mark, like a burn, cut deep into the flesh. It was all inflamed and angry-looking.

"Ow!" I said.

"It hurt a lot," Almay said. "Still does. I was wearing shorts, and Jordie warned me. He said, don't let your leg touch that—whatever he called it, this hot metal thing on the motorcycle—but my leg did touch it, by accident. And I got burned. That's why I'm wearing pants. If Mama saw, she'd whup me good."

"You mean you were on his motorcycle?" I said.

She pulled down the leg of her pants. "Yup. And I got to wrap my arms around his waist and hold him tight."

I just shook my head. I couldn't imagine being dumb enough to go off with a boy from the migrant camp on a motorcycle, especially if the boy was Jordie. But at the same time, I wondered what it would be like to hold on to a boy like that.

I moved to the edge of the porch and picked up a stick. I poked it around in the dirt, thinking about how I don't really like any boys. I guessed I would someday, because I know that practically everybody does, eventually. But how come Almay already did?

"Look at this," I said, turning over a squirming brownish bug. "A June bug."

It was on its back, its legs wiggling like crazy in the air.

Almay moved over and sat down on the steps beside me, and Vanessa sat beside me on the other side. Almay leaned forward, brushing her hair up toward her face and away from her neck, wiping the sweat from the back of her neck and her shoulders. I could smell her smell then, sweaty, but kind of sweet, too, a smell like Geneva—earthy, grown-up.

She looked down at the bug. "Jordy found a praying mantis last week," she said. "He pulled off its legs."

I turned the June bug over so it was on its feet, then watched while it rocked and staggered a little, then crept away. I imagined it going home, telling its mama how lucky it was that it was me who had found him, not Jordie.

"Jordie's sick," I said.

"He's OK," Vanessa said.

I looked at her, surprised. Even though neither of us had ever said it out loud, I'd always been pretty sure that Vanessa didn't like Jordie any more than I did.

"Tell her what he's going to do, Almay," Vanessa said.

Almay shook her head. "No. He's not going to do anything," she said. "So leave it alone." She stood up. "Want to play boyfriends? You two be Jordie, and I'll be me. We can kiss."

I made a face at her. Last summer all three of us had tried pretend kissing, just like we had tried imitating Mama's looks, seeing what it was like. But we always burst out laughing.

"No!" I said. "I'm not being Jordie. And *what's* he not going to do?"

"We don't have to do real kisses, like on the mouth," Almay said, ignoring my question. "We could just kiss hands. We can practice."

"No!" I said. "I don't want to practice. And I don't want to kiss."

"Why not?" Vanessa said. "What's the matter with boys?"

"Nothing's the matter with boys!" I said, turning to her. "Why? Are you in love, too?" Because I thought suddenly of what she had just said about Jordie, that he wasn't so bad, and I wondered if maybe she was in love with him, too.

"No, silly," she said. "But Jordie's sweet on Almay. He's going to get her into the Montanas' pool. All three of us."

"He's not, so stop it," Almay said. "And anyway, Vanessa, you are too in love. You told me."

"I did not!" Vanessa said. "I just said Matthew Winkler was cute." She turned to me. "He was with his mama at church Sunday, and she was talking about you saving James. Everybody was talking about it. Matthew kept smiling at me from behind his mama's back, and he's just cute. So let's practice. Then we can be like—*ready.*"

"Ready?" I said. "For kissing?"

Vanessa smiled.

I shook my head at her, disgusted. And then I saw her look at Almay and Almay look back and both of them rolled their eyes.

Suddenly I felt mad, mad and confused and mean-feeling. The whole world was crazy. Mama was crazy. My friends were suddenly boy crazy. Jordie, who was mean as a snake, was now a good guy. And Almay could be in big trouble, too, not only because of being in love, but because of Jordie being white. And what could he possibly do about the Montanas' swimming pool? I felt tears spring up to my eyes and I blinked hard, pushing them back. Maybe I was just tired. I'd been up since before it was even light this morning, and then I had that whole scene with Mama and the hotel, and then there was the ride home and . . .

And how could you be ready for any of this stuff? How could you be ready for anything?

"I don't like playing stupid stuff," I said. And even though I knew I probably wasn't being fair, I stood up. "I'm going home," I said. "If you two want to play kissing games, you can kiss each other without me."

Ten

Next morning when I woke, the sun was full up in the sky. I could tell by the sounds in the house that Geneva was already at work in the kitchen, and Daddy had probably already left for the store. In fact, it was most likely that Daddy had slammed the front door when he went out, and that had awakened me. A mockingbird was singing furiously in the tree just outside, one song after another, after another, as if it had to run through its whole chorus of songs before the sun had cleared the treetops. A kingfisher made its trilling sound, and I knew that meant it was about to dive for a fish in the creek out back. I always wonder about kingfishers, the way they trill just before diving, and how come the fish doesn't get warned away when it hears that sound. Sparrows and wrens were chirping in the little bushes out back, so close it seemed I might reach out and touch them.

I lay listening to them, watching the gauzy white curtains blow in and out with the motion of the fan, thinking about my friends, about Mama, about everything that had happened in the past week. It was worrisome about Mama. But it was plain annoying about my friends. It's not that I don't like boys at all, because I do. Sort of. But Jordie was dangerous. And Almay was plain dumb to get on his motorcycle. And though I wanted desperately to get into the Montanas' pool, I didn't want anything to do with Jordie. After a bit, I got up, pulled off the T-shirt that I'd been sleeping in, and stood looking at myself in the mirror. I'm awfully skinny, and I have freckles everywhere, even on my back and chest, some really big freckles. I sometimes think I could have a real tan if the freckles all ran together. My hair is thick and straight, but kind of a nothing, sandy color, sort of like a field mouse, although it gets prettier by this time of midsummer, when it gets streaks from the sun. My eyes are OK enough, I guess, green and big—big as frog eyes, Geneva says, though I don't think that's much of a compliment.

I turned sideways in the mirror, looking to see if my breasts were beginning to poke out any. They weren't. Of course. I'd checked yesterday. I check every day. Almay definitely has breasts and curves, and even Vanessa, I noticed, is getting little bumps popping out under her shirt. And I've noticed something else, too: boys notice if you have breasts or don't have them.

Well, I didn't have them. And I didn't care.

Well, maybe I cared a little. I even told Geneva once that I knew I'd never get to be pretty or grown-up looking, not ever.

Geneva just said, "Don't you worry yourself none. One of these days, you'll be right pretty. And you'll have all the curves you're supposed to have."

"I don't want curves," I'd said. Although of course, I did.

Anyway, now it was clear that no curves had appeared magically overnight, and I pulled on my shorts and a shirt, then went off to the bathroom to wash up.

I had just come out and was halfway downstairs, when I

heard Mama call my name.

"Missy?"

I turned around and looked up.

"Mama?" I said.

"In here," she answered.

The door to her room was partway open, and she was peeking at me from behind it.

"What, Mama?" I said.

"Come here," she said, beckoning to me.

I went back up the stairs and into her room, smelling that familiar smell of orange that seems to linger around Mama. "What, Mama?" I said again.

She pulled me inside, then shut the door behind me. "I want you to look at something," she said.

She went to her dressing table, picked up a book, then came and handed it to me. "Have you seen this before?" she asked.

I turned it over in my hands. It was her prayer book, small and blue, with words printed on the cover in gold—at least, they used to be gold, but now they were mostly worn away. It said, "A Mother's Manual." I've seen Mama pray with this forever.

"Yes," I said, handing it back to her. "It's yours. Why?"

"You've seen it before?" Mama asked again.

"Of course!"

"Where?" she said.

I shrugged. "Here. Everywhere. You always have it. Why?"

"Look at who wrote it," Mama said.

She handed it back to me, and I turned it over in my hands. "Francis Coomis, SJ," I read. "It was written by a Father Coomis."

"Ha!" Mama said triumphantly, like she had caught me out in a lie. "*I* wrote it! I wrote it. But I never told anybody. And now this Father Coomis is trying to steal my idea, and he's probably publishing it all over the place and making the money off it, getting rich on *my* prayers!"

"*You* wrote it?" I said. Because for a minute, I actually believed her. Except then, of course, I realized differently.

"Of course, I wrote it," she said. She took it back from me. "But don't tell Mimi," she said, waggling a finger at me. "She'd be terribly jealous if she knew how successful I was."

I took a deep breath. "OK. I won't tell," I said.

"Promise?" Mama said.

"I promise, Mama," I said.

"You're a good girl," Mama said softly. She turned away from me and went to the window. There's a big cushy chair there, and she settled herself in it. It's her favorite place, and lately she has been sitting there by the hour, just staring out, thinking whatever it is she thinks.

She hadn't dressed yet, and with the sunlight streaming through the window, I could see through her thin nightdress. Mama's tiny, always has been, but now she looked especially thin, fragile-seeming, even, her bones like tiny bird bones. Her collar bones and shoulder bones stuck out, and the hollow of her neck was so deep you could put a stone or a little pool of water there. I imagine that if she stayed very still, the water or stone would just stay put. A kind of aching feeling happened inside me.

"Mama!" I said suddenly, softly. "Mama, why don't you come out and play with Vanessa and Almay and me today?"

Mama turned to me, her eyebrows up.

"Remember?" I said. "Remember how you used to? We can sit on the steps and talk, or maybe even walk to Daddy's store. Or maybe—remember how you and Vanessa and Almay and me played dominoes? And sometimes, you played the piano and Almay sang for us? Want to do that again?"

Mama looked away. "I was better then, wasn't I?" she said softly.

"No, Mama!" I said. "You were the same. You *are* the same. You're fine. So won't you? Won't you come outside? Or— maybe we could write stories. Remember how you used to do that? We wrote a play that Almay got to sing in?"

And then I thought of what she had just said about her prayer book, and I wanted to bite my tongue. "We can do something, OK?" I said.

"Don't worry," Mama said. "I'll work it out. I'll make sure I get what's owed to me."

She turned away from me and picked up her rosary beads from the little round table alongside the chair. She began fin- gering the glass beads, her lips moving in silent prayer. Her eyes got that glassy look, the way they do sometimes, fixed on something outside the window, something in the far distance, it seemed—or maybe it was nothing—maybe just something that only she could see. But I could see that tears suddenly trembled at the edges of her eyes.

I stood watching her, feeling that aching inside of me, my heart almost hurting inside my chest. I wanted to say, "What, Mama? Why are you crying?" But I bit it back.

There was no sense asking. She might not even know. She probably didn't know. But this I knew: she hadn't written that little prayer book, and nobody had stolen her prayers, her words. If she was crying over that—well, what could I do?

I left the room quietly and went downstairs, still feeling that ache inside. Mama didn't mean to be crazy; I knew that. She tried so hard. I knew that, too. It's why we'd gone away, all secret-like.

I wondered: could I have done anything different? Could I have made the week better for her? Should I maybe not have complained about not being allowed to go swimming? Would that have made a difference? I didn't know. I just didn't.

Eleven

I had a bowl of cereal in the kitchen with Geneva, then went out on the back porch to wait for Almay and Vanessa to come. It was another hot morning, one of those misery days when everything stuck to everything else—my legs to the porch steps, my shorts to my underwear, my underwear to my bottom. Even my hair felt hot. The crickets and locusts were chirping away, like they were real happy that it was going to be such a lousy day. Mama gets mad at locusts because she says that they cause the heat. But I know that all they do is report it.

I sat on the steps, looking down the lane, waiting for Almay. What could I do for Mama? If only I could get her to come away from that window, from sitting and praying—and crying. I wondered how Almay and Vanessa would feel if I said I wanted Mama to come do something with us. Maybe we could all go to a movie or something. We could just walk to the Majestic in town if there was anything good playing. Mama used to like movies.

After a little bit, I saw Almay coming up the lane, swinging a stick at the grasses and weeds that grow up along the road, raising clouds of dust as she came. She was wearing those long, flowy pants again, and her feet were bare. Her mama must have done her hair, because it was pinned up on top of her head, and I thought she looked really grown-up that way, almost like a princess. I waved to her when she was still a ways off, and she waved back, but she didn't hurry herself any. Not that I blamed her. It was too hot to walk, much less hurry.

She got to the porch and plopped herself down beside me. "I'm gonna die!" she said. "I bet it's a hundred degrees already."

"We could sneak off to Slow Pond and cool off," I said, even though, of course, I didn't mean it.

She didn't even bother to answer that. I wanted to ask about the Montanas' pool and if it was finished and all those things. But I didn't want to bring it up with Almay. I figured I could wait and ask Vanessa when Almay wasn't around.

"Where's Vanessa?" I said. "She's always here by now."

"She's going to visit her grandma today."

"Rats! For how long?"

"Just the morning."

For a while we just sat there side by side silently. Almay was humming something softly, that deep, rich sound that comes out of her, sounding like she is a grown person, not just a kid. Suddenly, she turned to me. "Are you going to teach the little kids to swim?" she asked.

I didn't look at her, but I felt this little skip in my heart. "Who told you that?" I said.

"Doesn't matter," she said. "Are you?"

"No," I said. "Probably not."

"Why not?"

I just shrugged.

"If I got to go in a pool, I'd go, even if you couldn't," she said.

"You would not!" I said.

"Bet?" she said.

"Bet," I said.

Almay made a face. "Like if you don't go in the pool, that's going to do anything for me?"

"I'm not doing it for *you!*" I said.

"Then?" she said.

I didn't answer.

Almay moved away from me, leaving a space between us on the step. "Right. You're doing it for yourself," she said. "So you can think you're such a goody-goody."

"You are such a jerk!" I said. "How do you know what I'm thinking?"

She didn't answer. For a long while we were both quiet. What we were talking about was dangerous. Almay's her color and I'm my color, just like Geneva says.

After a while, I took a deep breath. "Can you keep a secret?" I said.

Almay shrugged.

"My mama," I said. "I think my mama's crazy."

"That's a secret?" Almay said. "The lane people know that. Girl, you should have heard the talk while you were gone!"

"What'd they say?"

"What didn't they say?" she said.

"Tell me," I said. Not because I cared that much. But we were getting back to a safe place.

"They said she's crazy, of course," she said. "My uncle Peach says he's never seen anyone crazier, not even in California. Except maybe for Uncle Maxwell."

"I remember him," I said. "Last summer. They came in an ambulance for him."

She nodded. "And they wrapped him up in a coat thing with the sleeves that tied in the back."

"Yeah," I said. "And your mama wouldn't let me go watch."

"It was something else!" she said. "That whole morning, he kept saying there were crumbs climbing up all over him. They jumped out of his biscuits and were attacking him, and he was clawing at them like crazy. These ambulance men came and took him away in a street jacket."

"Straitjacket, you mean," I said.

"That's what I said," she said. "But then he died."

"From what?" I said.

She shrugged. "Being crazy, I guess," she said.

"Well, Mama's not that crazy!" I said. I swear, Almay has no sense at all. Like I wanted to hear about somebody dying from being crazy. Although in a way it was sort of good to know there was someone crazier than Mama.

"You know what?" Almay said. "Maybe we could ask Uncle Peach about your mama."

"What would he know?" I said.

"Lots of things!" Almay said. "He put spiderwebs on a cut of mine once and it all healed up in . . . Oh!" She looked down at her leg. "Maybe he could fix my burn. Come on. Let's go down the lane. We'll ask him."

"You think so?" I said.

"Yeah," she said. "Why not?"

Why not? Because I'm not supposed to go down the lane. But Geneva had let me go yesterday, so I figured she couldn't get too mad if she found out I went today, too.

Besides, Almay was reaching to help me up. And she was holding out her hand to me. I waited just a second.

And then I took it.

Twelve

We walked slowly, looking at the fields wilting
in the sun, the dust rising off the path. One of the lane dogs
was chasing a bird that had just flown up from the grasses.
It gave up on the bird, and tagged along behind us, its
tongue hanging out, its fur all wet and matted, like it had
rolled in the creek and then in the dirt. I stopped to pet it,
and Almay bent down, too.

"Poor dog," she said. "You're so hot."

"Remember that summer when we had a pet show?" I
said.

Almay smiled and nodded.

We continued on, Almay humming some sort of tune,
the dog trailing along after us. At the foot of the lane, the
houses were spread out in a row, like a little toy town, one
house right up close to another, all of them leaning toward
the ground a bit. We passed a rusted-out school bus that
someone was living in, passed a couple of chickens that
were pecking around in the dirt. No people, though. I fig-

ured they were all at work or else hiding inside from the sun.

At the end of the row of houses, there was a slightly bigger house with a sign painted on the front in washed-out blue letters: STORE. That's all it said, not what kind of store or anything.

The front door was standing open, and inside it was dark. But even from there, I could feel a bit of cool air seeping out. The dog went up the steps and settled himself on the porch in the shade, panting.

Almay went up on the porch and called in the open door, "Uncle Peach?"

There was no answer. She popped her head inside and looked around. "Not here," she said. "Let's try the square. He sometimes visits down there."

What she called the square was just a dusty, flattened-out place, the earth all beaten down, and a rail with a hitching post, from when people used to have horses. There are no horses now, but there was a motorcycle locked up there—about the only thing you ever see locked up around here. But no Uncle Peach.

"Let's try the shed," Almay said.

Without waiting for my answer, she headed across a field. I followed her through weeds and grasses, to a rickety shed kind of thing in the middle of what looked like a junkyard.

There was every imaginable kind of thing back there—rusted-out tractors, parts of cars, an old refrigerator with the door off—Geneva once told us that doors should be taken off abandoned refrigerators so that children couldn't suffocate inside—tires, a washing machine, busted-up lawn chairs. There was even an old Greyhound bus lying tilted over, so that the dog on the side looked like it was running lying down.

I could hear the rhythmic sound of something squeaking—like a wheel turning or a motor running—and mixed in, the sound of someone whistling.

Almay took a deep breath and smiled. She grabbed my hand. "Jordie," she whispered.

Suddenly, the sounds stopped, and someone stepped out from the shadows of the shed.

It was Jordie, and he was holding something in his hand. At first, I thought it was a bird. And then I looked closer—and it *was* a bird. A sparrow? No, a mockingbird, a little gray baby mockingbird, with a long tail that hung down in back. Usually mockingbirds' tails are flipping around, looking lively, but this bird's tail was hanging straight down, like it was sad. And it lay on his hand, one eye looking at us—wild-looking, I thought— its head trying to turn this way and that, but feeble-looking.

Jordie looked up from the bird and nodded at us. "Hey," he said. "Lookit this. I was just going to get rid of it."

"Where'd you find it?" Almay said.

"Under my bike in the shed," Jordie explained. He held the bird up, its one wing torn-looking, the feathers drooping down just like the tail was drooping.

"Its wing is broken," I said.

"Like I didn't know?" answered Jordie. "A cat must've caught it and dragged it in."

"What are you going to do with it?" I asked.

Jordie smiled at me, but then he quick shut down his smile, pulling his lips down over his teeth, like to hide them. But not quick enough. I saw the gap where there was a broken tooth in front, broken right in half. I didn't remember him having broken teeth, but then, I had probably never looked at him up close.

I had a sudden scary thought—about him pulling the legs off the praying mantis.

"We could dig up worms," I said quickly. "Birds like worms. And then it could get stronger, and when its wing heals, it could fly away."

"And seeds," Almay said. "They eat seeds."

"Nah, it wouldn't eat," Jordie said.

"Would, too," I said. "Bet."

"Would not," Jordie said.

"So what are you going to do with it?" Almay said. She was tilting her head and smiling at Jordie, a look I'd never seen before. It reminded me suddenly of Mama's looks—and I remembered how hard Almay and I had worked at that kind of look. And how we had failed. At least, until now.

Jordie shrugged. "I guess I'll wring its neck," he said. He smiled at us, a sly kind of smile, his lips still together as if he was trying to hide his broken teeth. "You girls want to watch?"

"No!" I said. "Give it to me."

"Why? If you put it down, a cat will just get him."

"I'm not going to put it down. I'm going to take care of it." I held out both hands. "Give it to me."

Jordie didn't move. He just looked down at the bird in his hand, still smiling that little, sly smile. "It's just a bird," he said quietly, like he was talking to himself.

Almay swung around to face him, her face flushed, like she was about to speak. But then she turned and looked away without saying anything.

"I want it," I said again, my hands still reaching for it. "Give it to me."

"Make me!" Jordie said.

Suddenly, I was scared. Jordie couldn't do anything to us. We were practically in Almay's backyard. But he could kill the bird, and . . .

"Here! Take it!" Jordie said suddenly. He thrust the bird into my hands hard, so hard that I was afraid he'd squashed it.

But it wasn't squashed. It was scared, though, and I could feel its heart beating so hard that it almost scared me, its whole body trembling. And now that I had the bird, I hadn't the slightest idea what to do with it. I just stood there and felt it peeing on my hands, and I wanted to set it down. But of course I couldn't.

Jordie was wiping his hands on his pants. "Dirty bird," he said. "It pooped on me."

He turned and started back into the shed, leaving Almay and me just standing there.

"Jordie!" Almay called out. "What are you doing in the shed?"

He didn't answer.

"Jordie?" Almay called again. "What're you doing in there?"

"Fixing my bike," he called back.

"Can we watch?" Almay called.

He shrugged, but he didn't stop or turn around. "No law against it, I guess."

Almay turned back to me. "Want to?"

I shook my head. "How can we? We have to take care of the bird."

"Oh."

"We have to dig up worms. And find a box for it and stuff."

"You can do that. Can't you?"

I didn't answer.

"That's all right, isn't it?" she said. "I'll catch up with you later, OK? You have to go home for dinner, anyway."

I just looked at her.

She looked back, but I could see her face was flushed, embarrassed-looking.

I stared at her for a minute longer, then turned away. Twice today we'd been fighting. Twice today she'd been a jerk.

Well, I didn't care. I had the bird, its little wings fluttering feebly, its heart beating violently against my hands.

"Don't worry, little bird," I whispered. "I'll take care of you myself."

Thirteen

I walked slowly back to the house, trying to calm the wild feelings that had welled up inside me. And the poor bird—its heart was beating so fast I could hardly believe how fast. Could it die from being so scared?

"It's OK, little bird," I told it quietly. "I won't hurt you. But I can't put you down because a cat will get you. Or even a rat or a ferret or one of those things. You have to be able to fly to be safe."

Its head wasn't even swiveling toward me anymore, like it was just too tired. Its eyes were closed, too, but I knew it was alive, could feel that heart going like crazy.

"We're almost there, little bird," I said, when we were out of the lane and up to the backyard. "Almost there. And then I can put you in a box, and you won't be so scared. I'll find food for you, too."

I wondered if I could maybe find a nest, one that other birds had left empty. Sometimes you see nests just hanging in treetops. I looked up and around me and saw that someone was waving to me from up by the house. Vanessa!

"Hey, Missy!" she called. "What do you have there?"

"Come look!" I said.

She came to me, then bent over my hands. "Oh, a bird," she said. "But look at its wing: it's broken! Where'd you find it?"

"Almay and I were down the lane. Jordie had him."

"Jordie?"

"He was going to kill it."

She shuddered. "Where's Almay?"

"Still with Jordie. She stayed down there with him."

"Why? He was going to kill the bird!"

I shrugged. "You know her," I said. "You know how she is about Jordie. He's back in the shed fixing his bike and she's back there making eyes at him."

"Her mama better not find out," Vanessa said. "What are you going to do with the bird?"

"Get it a nest or something. A box. And we got to find it food, too."

Together we climbed the back porch steps. Vanessa held open the screen door for me, and we went in.

It was dark inside, after the bright sun, and for a minute, I couldn't see anything. "Geneva?" I called.

"Don't have to yell," she answered, and I realized she was right there, bending over the cutting block under the window, moving a chopping knife up and down, up and down over a row of vegetables, sending little bits flying every so often.

"Geneva," I said, "I need a box." I held out the bird for her to see. "See? It's hurt. Its wing is broken."

Geneva put down the knife and came around the board to Vanessa and me.

Suddenly, she began flapping her hands and moving fast toward me, shooing me out the door. "Lordy!" she said.

"Lord 'a mercy on us. Get it out of here this minute. This minute!"

"It's just a baby bird," I said. "It needs food and water and a box for a while."

"Out of here!" she said again. "Child, don't you know it's bad luck to bring a bird into a house? Lord, what will happen to us now?" She crossed herself, then fingered this little charm she wears on a string around her neck.

"You're silly," I said. Yet the way she was acting made me a little nervous. Geneva's always a little grumpy and annoying, but now she seemed actually scared. But how could a bird be bad luck?

"My grandma has a parakeet," Vanessa said.

"I don't care what your grandma has!" Geneva said. "Wild birds bring bad luck. Real, real bad luck. Now go on. Out of here."

The whole time she was saying this, she was backing me up to the door.

"I'm not taking it outside," I said. "I need a box for it."

"Out!" Geneva said, pointing. "I'll bring the box out."

"A cat will get it if it's on the porch," I said.

But even so, Vanessa and I scurried on out to the porch. I can't ever remember seeing Geneva so upset—not even the day we sneaked off to Slow Pond.

In a minute, Geneva was back on the porch with a small wooden box, the kind Daddy brings eggs home in. There was some sawdust in it, left from the egg packing. "Here," she said. "Now I don't want to see it back inside. Lord knows what kind of bad luck you've brought down on us this day."

"That's just a superstition," I said. "Sister Stella said superstitions are bad."

"*Birds* are bad," Geneva said. And she went back into the house, slamming the screen door behind her, muttering under her breath.

Carefully, I set the bird down in the box.

It just lay there like a dead thing, not even twitching. But I could still see that racing heart beating against its breast.

"What about cats?" Vanessa whispered.

I looked around the porch. "I'll put it up high here on the ledge where the clothespins are."

"A cat can climb," she said.

"It would need wings to get up that high," I said. "But look. The bird still hasn't moved."

"It's probably just tired," Vanessa said, peering into the box. "Maybe after it sleeps, it will be better."

"Yeah," I said. "I'd be tired, too, from being so scared."

"Should we try digging up worms?" Vanessa said.

I nodded. "But after dinner. We'll get bread crumbs and water, too. Let's go in now."

Back inside, Geneva was at the stove, stirring vegetables in a pot, and a wonderful smell was coming up from it, like pot roast. She looked up at us when we came in.

"Wash your hands good," she said. "Birds have mites. And where'd you get that bird from anyways?"

I went to the sink and turned on the faucet. I'm not real good at lying, never have been. I just sucked in a deep breath. "What's mites?" I said.

"Bugs!" she said. "Get cleaned up good because your daddy will be home for noon dinner in about five minutes. You look a wilted mess."

"I am wilted," I said.

I put my hands under the running water, looking for bugs. There was mud and streaks of stuff from where the bird had peed on me and teensy little scratchy marks from its claws. I didn't see any things that looked like bugs, though, not even under my fingernails, but I scrubbed with the nailbrush just to be sure.

Vanessa stood beside me, scrubbing her hands, too, though she hadn't even touched the bird.

"Where'd you get that bird from, anyway?" Geneva asked again. And then, like she'd just realized something, she added, "You had a fight with Almay or something?"

"No, ma'am," I said.

"Where is she?" Geneva asked. "I saw you two go off together."

Vanessa slid a look at me.

Well, even if I was mad at Almay, I wasn't going to tell on her. "She's around," I said.

"Around *where*?" Geneva said.

I turned off the water, took a towel and dried my hands, then handed the towel to Vanessa. I shrugged. "I don't know," I said. "She probably went home, I guess."

For a minute, Geneva didn't say anything. And then she said, "If you girls had a fight, you better make it up. There's a lot of summer left to be sitting around all by your lonesomes."

I heard footsteps on the front porch, and then heard the screen door open and close. I also thought I heard a car pulling away. Daddy? It couldn't be Daddy. It was only five to twelve. Daddy comes in at 12:04, exactly, and he walks besides.

I looked at Geneva. She was frowning at the clock.

"Now who could that be?" she said.

I shrugged. "Daddy?"

Geneva shook her head. "Oh, Lordy!" she said. "The one day in his life that he's early, and I still have to do that salad. Now out a my way, you two. I swear, I never saw two skinny girls take up so much room!"

It's true that Vanessa and I are both skinny. But it's also true that Geneva is fat. She's the one who took up most of the room. But I surely wouldn't ever say that.

I heard footsteps again, someone moving through the dining room. Daddy would be sitting down with his paper. Mama? Had Mama gone out and then come in?

"Where's Mama?" I said to Geneva.

"Up in her room, probably. She'll be down soon enough."

Geneva hustled to the refrigerator and took out the makings of a salad. "Vanessa," she said, "you're welcome to stay if it's all right with your mama."

Vanessa looked at me. "It's all right?"

"'Course," I said. Vanessa should know by now that Geneva makes the rules around here.

"I'll run home and ask," Vanessa said.

But before she could move, the door between the kitchen and the dining room swung open.

We all looked up, and my heart began thudding furiously in my throat.

I looked quickly at Geneva, then looked away. She had been right, right about the bird. Right about the bad luck I had brought down on the house. Because standing in the doorway—straight and tall and starched and squinty-eyed—was Mimi.

Fourteen

Well, of course, Vanessa didn't stay to dinner.
Mimi just shooed her on her way. And when Daddy came
in—at 12:04 exactly—and Mama still wasn't down in the dining room, Mimi went upstairs after her. A few minutes later,
the two of them came downstairs together, Mimi holding
Mama tightly by the arm. And then all four of us sat down to
dinner.

Daddy rang the buzzer that's on the floor under his
chair, and Geneva came in with the food. She set the plat-
ters down hard on the table, then turned and went back
through the swinging doors. She didn't say a word, not
one, and she almost always says something—some com-
ment about the food, about what sauce went on what,
about how fresh the vegetables were or how much the
meat cost. Geneva isn't ever shy about talking about food
and cooking. Now, though, she didn't speak and she
didn't look at any of us, either. I figured I knew why, of
course: Mimi.

Daddy began serving everyone, and as he did, he smiled warmly at Mimi.

"This is a nice surprise," he said.

Mimi just nodded.

"Will you be staying with us for a while I hope?" Daddy said.

"As long as necessary," she said. She looked over at Mama. "It's only what any Christian would do."

Daddy raised his eyebrows. "Oh?" he said. He managed to make it sound polite, but I could tell he was surprised and maybe a bit annoyed, too.

"Yes," Mimi said. "One knows when one is needed."

I stared down at my plate, trying to suppress the urge to laugh out loud. I had forgotten how sometimes Mimi talks about herself in the third person—"One," instead of "I."

Daddy nodded and continued carving and serving.

"You're wondering how I knew," Mimi said.

Daddy looked up at her. He didn't answer, just smiled.

"One has one's ways," she said.

Daddy was silent a moment, and then he just nodded again. "Well," he said, "you're always welcome. I hope you know that. And I hope you'll stay as long as you wish."

Well, if it was me, I would have said, *one* isn't needed and, actually, *one* isn't welcome, either. But of course, I didn't. A little part of me even thought that maybe Daddy didn't mean it, either. But he's far too polite to say so.

After a few minutes, we were all served, and we said the blessing and everyone began to eat. Everyone but Mama, that is. She didn't eat, not a thing, just sat staring down at her plate. After a minute, I saw her looking up at me, a kind of pleading look.

"What, Mama?" I said quietly, leaning close to her. "What's wrong?"

"There's nothing *wrong* with your mama," Mimi said.

"Nothing that a firm hand won't fix."

She turned to Mama. "Now eat up!" she said. She picked up Mama's fork and handed it to her. "I want to see you eat everything on that plate."

Mama took the fork Mimi had handed her, but she didn't do anything with it. Just held it in her hand. And her hand was trembling.

I looked at Daddy, but he wasn't looking back. He was eating silently, his head bent over his plate. A few minutes later, he looked at Mama. He wiped his mouth with his napkin, then pushed his chair back and stood up. He came around the table, leaned over Mama and said something softly, too softly for me to hear. Mama nodded, and she stood, not looking at Mimi, not looking at me. Daddy put his arm around her.

"She'll eat later," Daddy said. "I'm taking her upstairs. She needs her rest."

When they were out in the hall, Mimi looked at me. "She needs a good spanking; that's what she needs," she said.

Suddenly, it was all I could do to keep the words from exploding out of me. How dare she say that? How dare she think she knew what Mama needed—like Mama was still a five-year-old or something.

I put my fork down and tried to calm myself. I looked at my hands, glad suddenly that I had scrubbed them clean. But then I remembered what Geneva had said, that I looked wilted. I wished I had had time to brush my hair and splash water on my face.

"Where were you this morning?" Mimi asked, as if she had been thinking exactly what I'd been thinking. "You look untidy. That's no way to come to table."

I held out my hands, my nice clean hands. "I was with Almay and Vanessa. And I was just washing up when you got here," I said. "I only got to my hands."

"Is that why were you in the kitchen?" she asked.

I thought of telling about the bird, but then thought better of it. "No," I said. "I was there—just because."

"Because why?" she said.

Because it's none of your business. But like always with Mimi, I think one thing inside my head and say something else out loud. I also remembered what Mimi had said at Thanksgiving—that I shouldn't spend so much time with Geneva. "No reason," I said.

Mimi pulled her mouth into a tight little line. "You know that Geneva is our maid?" she said.

I stared at her. Geneva is *our* maid? Like she *belongs* to us? She belongs to herself. I couldn't help it. "She doesn't *belong* to us," I blurted out. "And she's my friend!"

Mimi pressed her lips together. "How old are you?" she said.

"Twelve," I said. "Twelve and a half." *Like she didn't know that.*

"Almost thirteen," she said. "That's what I thought. You're old enough to be responsible now."

I am responsible.

"What your mother needs is for you to stay around here more," she said.

Around here more? I'm always here! Except when Mama takes me off somewhere. But again, those words were just in my head and I didn't say them.

"Your mama needs your company," Mimi said. "You're seldom here for her. Undoubtedly, that's why she ran away with you. She saw it as the only way she could get any time with you."

"That's not true!" I said. And then I said something rude, but I couldn't help it. "How could you know that? You're not here."

"Exactly," she said, smiling that tight-lipped smile. "And that's why I've come. I've spent a lot of time thinking and praying over this. And I have this all thought out. Now, this is what I'm thinking. I want you to spend your days with your mama from now on. I don't want you with Geneva in the kitchen, and I don't want you with that Almay person. Almay's not the best company for you, anyway. It was all right when you were both children, but not anymore. I don't see why your parents don't understand that. We'll work out a schedule. But I'll expect you to be here more. I'll talk it over with your father tonight."

I just stared at her. How dare she?

Mimi was staring out the window, nodding, like she was seeing it all in her head, fixing us all up—Mama and Daddy and me and Almay and Geneva.

"It will be good for you to help your mama," Mimi said, turning back to me. "It will be good for both of you. As I see it, you can read to her in the mornings. Then, when you bring her in to dinner, she'll have something to talk about. Maybe she'll want to talk about what you read that morning. After dinner, we can all take a nap. Then, after we freshen up, maybe we'll all go for a walk. We might even take in a movie. I'll make sure your daddy leaves us a bit of money every day."

She paused, and I noticed that she was breathing a little fast, maybe because she hardly ever says that many words all strung together at one time.

Just then, Daddy poked his head into the dining room. "Your mama's sleeping," he said, looking directly at me. "She's OK now. I'll see you at six o'clock."

"Fine, James," Mimi said, even though Daddy hadn't been talking to her. "That's fine." And she nodded, as if she was dismissing him.

I watched Daddy go into the hall. I could see him

reflected in the mirror that hangs by the coatrack, could see how he was putting on his hat and straightening his tie and coat sleeves. I saw him look up, and he saw me watching him in the mirror. He smiled at me and rolled his eyes. I knew what he meant—that he, too, didn't think much of Mimi. And then he went out, the screen door closing behind him with a little snicking sound.

When he was gone, Mimi rolled up her napkin, put it back into her napkin ring, then stood up. "It's time to have a talk with Geneva now," she said, and she started for the swinging door to the kitchen.

I watched her go. I was so angry. What did she think she'd have a "talk" about? But a little part of me was smiling, too. If she thought she was going to talk Geneva into anything, she was wrong. Mimi is bossy all right. But nobody can make Geneva do what she doesn't want to do. I thought of following Mimi into the kitchen, or at least of eavesdropping at the door, but then I suddenly remembered —my bird! I hadn't gotten it any water earlier!

But not through the kitchen.

I ran down the hall to the front door, then around the house to the back. I'd get water from the hose, maybe just dribble some into its mouth. I bet it would open its mouth. And then, as soon as Mimi was out of the kitchen, I'd go in and get bread crumbs and a dish for its water.

And maybe, if Geneva was in the right mood, maybe I could even plot with her about how the two of us could get around Mimi and her stupid plans.

Fifteen

The bird was alive—I could see its heart still beating fast against its breast feathers—but it didn't open its eyes or turn its head. I figured it was sleeping, probably. I found a little bottle cap by the garbage can and filled it with water, setting it in the box next to the bird. When it woke up, it could just turn its head and drink.

That finished, I turned to look in the window at Mimi and Geneva. Geneva was at the sink, her arms plunged deep into soapy water, and Mimi had just turned to go through the swinging door from the kitchen to the dining room. As soon as the door closed behind Mimi, I practically flung myself into the kitchen.

"Geneva!" I said.

She didn't turn to me.

"Geneva!" I said. "What did she tell you? Did she tell you what she planned? She wants me to take care of Mama! How am I supposed to take care of Mama?"

Geneva just shook her head.

"Did she tell you?" I said. "She wants me to stay with Mama. All day! I can't do that. And she terrified Mama at dinner. Mama was shaking! Mimi doesn't understand Mama at all."

Still Geneva didn't answer, just moved her shoulders slightly, shrugging.

"Who invited her?" I said. "I know Daddy didn't 'cause he was surprised. And Mama wouldn't!" I said.

"For sure I didn't," Geneva muttered.

"She says she won't even let me play with . . . my friends." I had started to say, "With Almay," but didn't want to hurt Geneva's feelings. "And," I went on, "she says I have to stay here with Mama. Did she tell you her plans?"

Geneva nodded. "Told me the same thing she most likely told you. You is to care for your mama. I is to care for this house. Period. End of story. Amen."

I took a deep breath. "And she told you I'm not supposed to come in the kitchen?" I said.

"That, too."

"Ha!" I said. "Like she can stop me."

"You listen here," Geneva said, turning suddenly and squinting up her eyes at me. "You do what she tells you."

"Do what she *tells* me? You mean like stay out of the kitchen? And stay with Mama all day?"

"I don't know about the Mama part. But you stays out of my kitchen till she's gone, however long that takes."

I just stared at her. Or rather at her back. Because she had turned away and was working at a pot, the stew pot, scrubbing it with steel wool, going round and round the bottom like the outcome of the war depended on how clean she got it.

"Geneva?" I said.

Nothing.

"Geneva?" I said again.

Still nothing. It was like she had gone stone-deaf.

"You put that down and talk to me, you hear?" I burst out. "You turn around and talk to me."

She didn't turn. And she didn't yell at me, either, or come to me and slap my face, like she maybe should have done, maybe would have done, another day.

I felt ashamed. But . . . .

"Geneva?" I said, tears running down my face. "Please? Please talk to me!"

She put down the steel wool, lifted the pot, held it to the light, then picked up a dish towel and began wiping it dry. She kept herself turned away from me. And she didn't say a word. Not one. She just polished up that pot with the dish towel, just like she'd done with the steel wool, and I could see she was breathing hard, her eyes slewed down. And she said nothing more to me, nothing at all.

I went to the back door, opened the screen, and crossed the porch. I reached up to the ledge and took down the box with my little bird in it. My hands were shaking so hard that I had to hold the box with both hands, just to keep from dropping it or from shaking it so bad that the bird fell out.

Carefully, I set the box on the railing and looked in.

The bird was still alive, lying on its side, and now its eyes were open, one eye watching me. It was watching me so carefully that I thought for a minute it would speak, would tell me exactly what it needed, what it was thinking. But of course, it didn't. It did blink twice, though, and I took it as a sign that it had seen me, that it knew I was there to help.

"I know how you feel," I whispered, picking up the little bottle cap and tilting it toward the bird's beak. "You're thinking you should be in a tree or flying around in the sun and singing, right? But here you are stuck in this little box, all injured and fragile-like, can't even hold your head up. What happened to you? Was it a cat?"

The bird closed its eyes, like it was too tired even to listen. But it did open its mouth just enough so that when I dripped in some water, it went into its mouth.

"Crackers," I whispered. "I'll get you crackers or bread crumbs next. Hold on. I'll be right back."

I stood studying the bird for a minute more, wondering. Should I go back into the kitchen? Or should I go dig up a worm or try to? I didn't want to go back into the kitchen. Geneva was mad at me. And I had been rude to her.

I looked around. The ground was gray and hard packed from the heat and sun and lack of rain. Even though Daddy kept the sprinklers going at night, by nine in the morning, everything was baked dry again. No way I could find a worm now. And anyway, the bird was probably too sick still to chew up a worm. I'd just have to get something from the kitchen.

I left the box on the railing, opened the screen door, and went back inside. Geneva had finished with the pots and was putting them away, bending over to put them in the lower cabinets. She straightened up and looked at me when I came in.

"Can I get some bread crumbs?" I said.

Geneva shook the dish towel out hard and hooked it over the oven door. Then she opened a cabinet, reached in for an old jelly jar. She unscrewed the lid and shook in some bread crumbs from a can. She handed the lid to me. "This should do," she said. "But if it don't work, you come to me. I'll help."

"You will?" I said, surprised.

She sighed and shook her head and gave me this look like she couldn't believe how dumb I was.

"But it's a wild bird," I said. "You said they were bad luck. And they are, aren't they? Look at what happened with Mimi."

"Hush with your smart mouth," Geneva said. "And that

bird ain't in my house now, is it?"

"No." I took a deep breath. "Geneva?"

"What now?"

I studied the jar lid. "I didn't mean to say what I said before."

"I knowed that."

"But don't you see?" I said, looking up at her. "It's all wrong. Mimi doesn't know what's right for Mama. I think she's going to make Mama worse."

Geneva just shrugged.

"So, couldn't you tell her it won't work? I can't be with Mama all day. I'm not giving up my friends. And I'm not staying out of the kitchen. Maybe we can both tell Daddy. I mean, Mama *is* getting worse. Even I can see that. So maybe Daddy'll think Mimi's plan is worth a try. But you're a grown-up. He'll listen to you. You can tell him that . . ."

"I can't tell him nothing," Geneva said.

"You can, too," I said.

Geneva just rolled her eyes at me. She began shaking her head again, back and forth, back and forth, looking at me in that way she'd just done, like I'm just too dumb to believe.

"Why not?" I said.

"Why not?" she said, her eyebrows up high.

"Yes," I said. "Why not? He'll listen to you because you're a grown-up. And because you've known Mama a long time and him, too, and . . ."

"And I got clothes to put on Almay's back," Geneva said quietly. "And shoes. And food on the table. And rent to pay. And when I can, flowers on my boys' graves."

I just looked at her.

"I takes care a you the best I can," she went on quietly. "Now you gots to do the best you can."

She turned away from me and picked up the can of Bon

Ami cleanser and began sprinkling it into the sink. Then she picked up a rag and started scouring out the sink, scouring it hard, round and round, round and round, her back to me.

I sucked in a deep breath and watched her work, bent over the sink like that, her body so big and bulky, so familiar; I knew every crease of it. I knew the feel of her better than I knew the feel of Mama, knew where her waist was wide, where a small roll of flesh rolled out over her apron top. I knew how soft and comforting her chest was, when I lay my head against her—at least, I used to when I was little. I knew her so well, knew what she said and even what she didn't say. And I knew what she was saying to me now— that she needed this job, that she couldn't afford to have Daddy, or even Mimi, get mad at her. But she was saying something else, and I knew that, too. She was saying her job was more important to her than I was—and that Almay was more important to her than I was, too.

I sighed. That made sense. It really did. But it made me feel kind of lonesome inside.

Sixteen

Notes in my secret notebook:

I need to find a way to help Mama. Mimi thinks she knows how—by bossing Mama around—but it isn't working. Mimi does not know how to be a mama. Maybe that's why Mama's sick so much, because her mama didn't do right by her.

Geneva knows how to be a mama. If I ever have a little girl, I'll know how to be a mama.

I can't wait to see my friends. In a few minutes, I'm sneaking out and we're going to meet by our tree.

It's been two days now, and my bird is still alive. I have to figure out how to get it to eat.

My throat hurts. I feel hot, like I'm getting a fever. Geneva will fuss at me if I get sick. She'll say it's the bird's fault. I wonder if it is.

Two more things: one, Geneva chases me out of the kitchen if I go in for a drink of water. She won't even speak to me. And two, yesterday I could hear the little kids jumping around in the swimming pool down the street. And I can't go.

I haven't figured out how to fix any of these things. But I will.

I finished writing in my secret book and then hid it in the box in my closet. With everything so nutty this summer, I had taken to writing out lists again in my notebook. I didn't think it really helped fix anything, but it seemed to help me inside my head when I wrote things down. I'd even been writing down some prayers; maybe because I don't much like the book that God is writing. So I write down the things I need and the things that I think He should do differently. But I wonder if He ever reads my books.

It was barely light out, the birds just beginning to waken, the house still and silent. From Mama and Daddy's room down the hall, I could hear the familiar little whistling, rumbly sound—Daddy snoring, even though he swears to everybody that he doesn't snore. Across the hall in the guestroom—Mimi's room—there was no sound. Her door was open, though, and earlier, when I'd gone down the hall to the bathroom, I'd peeked in. She was lying on her back in bed, perfectly still, her arms outside the covers, her head flat, not even using a pillow. She was so still and stiff, she looked like she was dead.

I tiptoed out of my room, holding my breath till I was past Mimi's door. I walked slowly and silently down the stairs, avoiding the third step from the bottom that squeaks, then stepped quietly through the kitchen and out the back door. I peeked into the bird's box, but the bird was still asleep. I noticed that its heart wasn't beating so fast against its breast the way it was yesterday. So maybe that meant it had calmed down a bit and was getting better. I didn't try to wake it up, though. I thought it probably needed to sleep.

The sun was just beginning to peep over the top of the trees. I walked slowly through the grass toward our tree—Willowware, where Almay and Vanessa and I have been meeting for as long as I can remember.

The grass was wet, and I was barefoot, one of the best feelings in the world—unless you happen to step on a snake or a slug. But, Lord, my throat was hurting. When I swallowed, it even hurt inside my ears. I'd better not be getting sick. Geneva would fuss. And Mimi would probably make me one of her horrid mustard plasters or something.

I reached our tree, ducked under the hanging branches, and sat down, my back against the trunk. I was the first one there, but after just a minute, I heard footsteps, and I peered out from beneath the branches.

But it was neither Almay nor Vanessa. It was Jordie! What was he doing out so early?

I leaned back again, not wanting him to see me. He walked silently past me, then headed down the lane toward where Almay lives. He was walking to the side of the path, in the grass, as though trying to stay quiet, not letting his feet crunch on the pebbles. He looked unsteady, as if he was tired or even sleepwalking. And he was filthy and rumpled. I wondered if he had even been to bed all night.

I watched him walk away sort of wobbly-like, till the lane bent and I couldn't see him anymore. What was he up to, sneaking like that?

After just a few minutes, I saw Vanessa coming toward me from the front of the house. And at about the same time, Almay came up the lane.

They both slipped beneath the long, hanging branches of the cottonwood and plopped down on the ground beside me.

"Did anyone see you sneaking out?" Vanessa said to me.

"Nope." I shook my head, then turned to Almay. "Did you see Jordie?" I asked.

"Jordie?" she said.

"Yeah, Jordie."

"When?" she said.

"Just now."

"No." She looked puzzled.

"I just saw him heading down the lane," I said.

"You did? I didn't see him. Was he looking for me?" Her eyes got all sparkly, and she began smiling.

I shrugged. "I don't know what he was looking for. But he looked awful—messy and tired, like he hadn't slept all night."

"He and his daddy do stuff at night," Almay said. "He told me they hunt sometimes."

"You still like him?" Vanessa asked.

Almay nodded. "Yeah. You still like Matthew Winkler?"

Vanessa wrinkled up her nose. "I never really *liked* him," she said. "I just said he's OK."

"Did not," Almay said. "You said he was cute."

Vanessa shrugged. "Don't you like anybody yet?" Almay asked, turning to me.

I started to say no. But then I remembered how they both thought I was dumb that day for not being interested in boys. "Well," I said slowly, "there's a boy at the hotel." The biggest, fattest lie I had ever told. Not that it was a lie exactly. I mean, there *had* been boys at the hotel.

"A boy?" Vanessa said. "You didn't tell us. What's his name?"

I looked up. A plane was flying low overhead with a heavy droning sound. "Wright," I said, picking a name out of the air. "Robert Wright."

"Did your mom know?" Almay asked. And then, before I could even answer, she said, "Oh, wait! I forgot."

She stood up and dug in the pocket of her shorts, then sat down again and handed me a small packet of waxed paper folded over and over, with something that looked like grass inside.

"From Uncle Peach," Almay said. "It's herbs. If you put them in hot water and make a tea from it, it will help your mama, he said."

"Thanks. Thanks for asking him."

I looked down at the bits of green in the package. Such a silly wish—or hope—that that little green stuff could make Mama better, make her come back to us. But it was worth a try.

"And look at this!" Almay said. She stuck out her leg, pointing to the place where the burn from the motorcycle had been. It was all smooth and pink and just a little puckered now, not angry and red anymore. "Uncle Peach put spiderwebs on it," she said.

"Wow! Was it gross?" I asked.

She shook her head. "No, it felt good."

"Remember the time we put on a play about a spider?" Vanessa said. "*Charlotte's Web?*"

I nodded. I did remember. "Mama wrote the script for us," I said. "And remember the Patriot Play and how she wrote a song for all three of us—'The Three Little Sisters?'"

"Yeah," Vanessa said. "Let's do that again. Only, let's do Peter Pan like we did in school last year."

"Yeah, and you'll be Peter Pan?" Almay said. It was kind of mean-sounding the way she said it. I knew why, too. As soon as Vanessa gets an idea, she has to be the star. And, of course, she had had the part of Peter Pan in that school play.

Vanessa just shrugged. "Why not? I already know Peter's lines."

"Then I'm Wendy," Almay said.

Vanessa shrugged. "Fine with me."

They were sort of glaring at each other and there was silence for a minute. "I don't want to do Peter Pan," I said. "I think we should do that patriot play. There were all those songs for Almay to sing."

They both turned to me.

"Can your mama still play the piano?" Almay said.

I shrugged. "Maybe."

"You think?" Vanessa said, doubtful-like.

I sighed. "No, not really," I said. "And, anyway, it won't work. You know that Mimi won't even let me out."

"Tell her to take her skinny self back to Georgia!" Almay said.

I looked at Almay. She had picked up a stick and was whacking the sand with it. I wondered if she knew Mimi didn't want me playing with her.

We were all quiet then. I lay back on the ground, my feet sticking out from beneath the tree's hanging branches, my head hurting something bad, my throat just burning up. But the grass felt good, cool and wet against my back. Almay began singing softly, one of the songs from *The Patriots*, and for a minute, it just felt so nice, sweet and quiet and restful. I could almost feel myself falling back to sleep.

Suddenly, the silence was broken by a roaring sound—a motorcycle. Jordie?

Yes. Jordie. He came zooming up the lane and stopped right by our tree. He got off his bike and peered under the tree branches. "Hey!" he said, and he came over to stand by us.

I sat up and wrinkled up my nose. He was streaked with mud, and he smelled horrid, like sweat and something else, too—something sweetish. And he was holding an open bottle of beer.

"Come here," he said to Almay, gesturing to her with the beer bottle. He didn't say it like he was asking—he said it like it was an order.

She stood up.

I couldn't help it. "Say *please* come here," I said.

"Who asked you?" he said to me. "Come here," he said again, motioning to Almay. "I got something to show you."

"What?" she said.

"Get on," he said. He ducked out from under the branches, stumbling a bit, then went to his motorcycle and patted the seat behind him.

Almay started over to the motorcycle, slowly. She looked at Vanessa and me, then back at Jordie.

"Almay," I said. "Don't. Your burn is just getting better. And you have shorts on."

"I'll be careful," she said.

"Come on!" Jordie said. "I ain't got all day."

"Where are you going?" Vanessa asked.

Jordie smiled at her, showing his broken tooth. "Going to show her a dead man."

"A *what?*" Vanessa said.

"A dead man," Jordie said.

"Right," I said, and I rolled my eyes at him.

"It's true," Jordie said. "You don't have to believe me, but it's true. Right back there in the creek. He's all swelled up."

Almay had climbed up on the motorcycle behind Jordie. Jordie began revving it up, spinning the engine, and fiddling with the handlebars, turning them back and forth.

Almay wrapped her arms around Jordie's waist.

Jordie revved the motor again, then looked over at us. His eyes were bloodshot, and he had that sleepy, unsteady look like I had noticed before. He was grinning, but even so, every time he blinked, the blinks seemed to get slower, like he was fighting to stay awake. He had tucked the beer bottle inside the front of his shirt, so that just the neck of it stuck out, right under his chin.

I scrambled to my feet. "Almay," I said, going over to the motorcycle. "Don't go. Get off."

She just looked at me. "Why?"

"Because!" I said. "I just don't think you ought to go."

"Nothing's going to happen," she said. "I'll keep my

leg away from that hot thing now."

"It's not just that!" I said.

"What are you—her mother or something?" Jordie said.

"Maybe," I said.

I turned to Vanessa. She had come to stand beside me, looking from me to Almay and Jordie and then back again. She looked a little scared.

"She shouldn't go," I said to Vanessa. "*You* tell her."

Vanessa frowned but she didn't say anything.

"Out of my way, you two, or I'll run you over," Jordie said. "You ready, Almay?"

He turned to look at her, and she nodded. But when he turned his head, I got another whiff of him—his dirty hair, his sweat, his foul, beery breath.

"Let's go, then!" Jordie said, just as I grabbed at Almay.

I flung my arms around her waist and pulled her back toward me—hard. She wasn't expecting it, and her arms came loose from around Jordie, her hands flying up in the air. But she stayed on the motorcycle. I tugged harder, both my arms tight around her middle. And then Vanessa was grabbing at her, too.

"Quit it!" Almay yelled.

But we didn't. We held on, and there was a jumble of bodies and tugging and huffing. And then Almay came flying off the motorcycle, arms and legs flailing every which way. And all three of us, Almay, Vanessa, and me, went tumbling backwards, landing in a heap on the ground.

In our struggle, the motorcycle had tipped. But Jordie stayed on it. He straightened it, revved it some more, then turned, glaring down at us in our heap on the ground. He shook his head and muttered something

under his breath—a swear. Then he revved up the motorcycle and roared on out of the pebbled drive.

It could not have been more than a second later that
we heard the sound: a screeching of brakes. Grinding of
metal on metal. Glass breaking. And then, a horrid thudding sound. And silence.

Seventeen

I was sick. Oh, Lord, I was sick.

No. Mama was sick.

I was just hot, hot and . . .

Was Mama sick like I was sick? Did her head hurt? Was she hot, burning up hot? It was dark inside my head. Was it dark in her head?

I didn't know, didn't know much about anything. I just lay in bed, my head burning up with fever, my legs and arms hurting so bad that I couldn't even bear to have a sheet over me.

Sometimes I woke from a fever sleep of nightmares to see Geneva sitting beside my bed, or Daddy, or Dr. Potts. Once even, it was Mimi. But I never saw Mama. And when I was awake enough to ask about Mama and about Almay and Vanessa—and about Jordie—they only said to rest. We'll talk later.

But I knew. I knew Jordie was dead. I'd seen him, his head smashed like a melon on the pavement, his eyeball lying on his cheek, the jagged beer bottle dripping blood onto his neck, the car he collided with hovering there in the middle of the street, the ambulances and how everything was rust-colored. I remembered it all, could see it all. But it kept getting mixed up with my hot dreams and the aching in my legs.

Every so often, I woke and Dr. Potts stuck me with a needle. And once—I was perfectly awake and knew I wasn't dreaming—I heard him say, "Possibly polio."

And I heard Daddy say firm and loud, "No. Scarlet fever. That's all it is."

"It's not polio," I said, clearly.

I saw them both look at me, startled.

And then I went back to sleep.

But even in my sleep, I knew. I knew it wasn't polio. It was just a pain inside me and I could see it, my heart all red and hot and my eyeballs bursting with the heat. But then they were Jordie's eyeballs, and they were falling out of my head, and it was all wrong.

The whole world was wrong. It was wrong, and nothing I could do would make it right. I could only sleep.

I don't know if it was a week or two weeks or a month that I lay there feverish. I only know that I woke up one morning, and I didn't hurt so much, and the sheet didn't feel like hot needles on my skin. Geneva was asleep in the chair beside me, and the birds were just beginning to waken, chirping and singing in the tree outside my window.

"I'm thirsty," I said.

Geneva's eyes opened.

"I'm thirsty," I said again.

Geneva blinked at me, sleepy-eyed. "What you say?" she said. "You say something, child?"

"I'm thirsty."

Geneva leaned over the bed and peered closely at me.

She reached out a hand, laid it on my forehead, left it there a moment. "Praise be to God," she said softly, closing her eyes. She put up a hand and touched the charm she wears on her neck, then crossed herself, all this before she opened her eyes. "Praise be to God."

She looked back down at me again, bending close, her face so close to mine. And I swear to you, I never saw eyes like that, eyes that you could drown in, dark, soft eyes. For just a minute, the whole world felt right.

"Mama?" I asked. "Where's Mama?"

"You're awake, child," she whispered. "Oh, Lord, we thought we'd lose you. Oh, Lord, Lord, Lord! Thank you, Lord."

I felt my eyes closing again, but I didn't want to go back to sleep. I needed to know about Mama. But I just couldn't fight off the sleep and I felt my eyes closing.

Maybe I slept an hour. Maybe it was just a minute. But when I awoke again, Geneva was right where she had been before, and there was a glass of water and some ice in a pitcher on the little table.

"Where's Mama?" I said.

Geneva just looked at me. "Child," she said, "I don't know if I'm s'posed to tell you this or not, but I'm telling you anyways. Your mama's gone away. It's a good enough place. She'll get better there."

"When?" I said. "When did she go? Where?"

"After you got sick," Geneva answered. "Couple weeks now. And I don't know where, but a place that'll do her good."

"When's she coming back? Soon?"

"Only God knows," Geneva said. She shook her head. "You know that."

She poured a glass of water and handed it to me. I took the glass, took a sip of water, then handed her the glass, and lay back against the pillows. It seemed like such a big effort to even hold the glass.

"Where's Daddy?" I asked.

"At the store. He been setting by you all night every night, though. Hardly slept a wink. He'll be so happy to see your fever's gone."

I thought about Mimi, but for some reason, didn't want to ask.

Geneva, though, she must have known. "Mimi's still here," she said. "Oh, she's here, all right. Most likely right now setting on the porch and praying. She don't do much else but set and pray. Don't see as it does her much good, though."

There was a hint of a smile in her voice, and it surprised me. I wondered if the two of them had made some sort of peace after I got sick. Not likely, though, I knew that.

I pushed back the sheet. "I have to go to the bathroom," I said.

Geneva reached out a hand and took my arm.

"I can do it," I said. "I'll help you," Geneva said. "Been helping you for weeks."

"You have?" I said.

She frowned at me. "You don't remember none of it, do you?"

I remembered Jordie. And the accident and . . . But I knew that wasn't what she meant.

I let Geneva help me walk down the hall, but I got into the bathroom and out by myself. Once I was back in my room, I saw that Geneva had fixed the sheets and fluffed up my pillows. I was glad to get settled in bed, and I rested my head back against the pillows.

"You done enough for one day," Geneva said. "Now you rest. I got to get dinner ready for your daddy. And, oh, wait till he sees you!"

She turned to go.

"Wait!" I said.

She stopped and turned to me.

I closed my eyes for a minute. How could I ask? What did I want to ask? How was Jordie? No, Jordie was dead. I knew that. How was Almay? And Mama—what made them take her away? The thoughts raced around, and I couldn't get hold of any of them.

"If you is going to ask about that Jordie and about Almay and Vanessa and that day, I ain't telling you nothing," Geneva said, as if she was mind reading.

I opened my eyes. "Why not?"

She looked away. "Because I'm not. So don't you ask."

"I know Jordie's dead," I said. "I saw him."

Geneva tilted her head at me. "You fainted dead away," she said.

"Maybe. But I saw him. I don't remember fainting, though."

"Well, you did." She sighed. "Lord a mercy on his soul; that's all I got to say."

"Is . . . are . . . are Vanessa and Almay here?"

"Here?" Geneva said. "'Course not. You been so sick child, we thought . . . No, of course, they not here."

"I didn't mean here, in this house. I meant . . . you know. *Here.*"

I meant had they been sent away—like that other summer. Had Geneva sent Almay to her grandma way down in Mississippi and had Vanessa gone to New Hampshire? Though why I would think that, I don't know, unless maybe because of that other summer when Mama went away and they went, too. Or maybe because my head was still confused.

"They's still around, if that's what you're asking," Geneva said. "Moping and snuffling. Almay, to look at her, you'd think her heart was broke."

It probably was. But I didn't say it.

Geneva didn't say anything, either, not for a full minute, at least. And then she said softly, "I know how she felt 'bout that boy. Almay doesn't know I know, but I do. You don't let on, now. Give her a chance to get over it, without worrying 'bout me and what I know or don't know. You hear?"

I nodded, though I was so surprised, I hardly knew what I was agreeing to. She knew? She knew that Almay was sweet on Jordie? How did she find that out? And did she know that Almay was almost on that motorcycle, too? All those thoughts were racing around inside my head. But when I spoke, I said something that had nothing to do with Almay or Jordie or Vanessa, either.

"I tried to help Mama," I said.

"I know," Geneva said, her voice kind, tender almost. "We all did."

I closed my eyes again.

"Your mama, she'll be back," Geneva said softly, after a minute. "God'll figure it out."

I didn't open my eyes. "Yeah? But when?"

"When He's ready," Geneva said. "He writes the book. You know that. Let's jes' wait and read it."

Eighteen

It was two days later, right after noon dinner, and I was feeling a lot stronger and better. Mimi had gone off to take her nap, and I was sitting on the floor in my room with Almay and Vanessa.

Geneva says my room is a strange kind of room for a child to have, but she's wrong. It's a perfect place for me. I keep it super neat, my stuffed animals, my books, my notebooks all in place, lined up neatly on my shelves and in my bookcase against the wall. It's my closet that's a mess, but it's a good mess in there. My bed is at an angle in the corner between two windows, so that I'm not turned to a wall no matter which way I turn over at night, because facing into a wall can make you feel claustrophobic, even in your sleep. With the windows open, the breeze floats in at night, and I can lie there and listen to the frogs and the crickets and cicadas and feel the moon lie on me some nights. I read once about moon madness, although I have no idea what that is. But when I was little, I used to think that maybe Mama got crazy from too much moonlight, and I used to close my curtains at night, so it wouldn't happen to me.

Now the three of us were sitting, not saying much, mostly moping. We had been talking about doing that play, the one we had been planning right before I got sick, or maybe having some sort of circus or carnival, but the conversation had just drifted to a stop. I think none of us really cared that much about it. We hadn't said a word yet about Jordie or the accident, each of us keeping our thoughts tight inside our very own heads. My thoughts weren't just about that, but about Mama, too. I wondered if either Almay or Vanessa knew why or how they had taken Mama away. I had asked Daddy, but all he said was that Mama had wanted to go away to get better. He didn't say if anything new had happened or what. But I had a feeling he wasn't telling me the whole truth. And, of course, I knew better than to even ask Geneva. I figured Geneva was blaming everything that had happened lately on my bird.

My bird? I jumped up.

"My bird!" I said. "What happened to my bird?"

Vanessa and Almay both just looked at me.

"I don't know!" Vanessa said.

"Come on. Let's go see," I said.

And all three of us raced down the stairs and out to the back porch. I hurried over to the back ledge where Vanessa and I had put the box with the bird in it. But there was no box. No bird.

"Maybe Geneva moved it," Vanessa said.

We burst into the kitchen. "Geneva?" I said. "My bird! What happened to my bird?"

"Flew away," she said, turning from the countertop where she had just laid a towel over a bowl, setting out some bread to rise. "Got all better and flew off. One morning, the box was just empty."

"Did you *see* it fly away?" I asked.

She just made a face at me. She looked at Almay and said,

"Get that hair off your face. You look about to wilt."

Geneva had this kind of sharp sound in her voice, the way she gets when she's worried. But there was a soft look in her eyes.

Almay had let her hair down from the topknot that Geneva sets it in each day. I thought she looked awfully pretty, her hair all curly around her face like a little bush. But she did look hot. She took a rubber band she had around her wrist and started to knot up her hair.

"How do you know it flew away? How do you know a cat didn't get it?" I asked Geneva. "Did you check?"

"You mean, did I go round the neighborhood asking all the cats, 'Did you eat up a sick little bird?'"

Vanessa giggled, but I just said, "You know what I mean!"

"I knowed what you mean, but no cat got it, because there weren't nothing there. No bones, no feathers, no nothing." She shook her head. "Well, Lord, I seen strange things in this life. But who would a thought it? A half-dead bird flying away."

I looked at Almay and Vanessa. They both shrugged.

"I guess it did, then," I said.

"And it didn't die," Almay said.

And the three of us went back upstairs to my room again. We went quietly, though, since Mimi was napping. And though Mimi hadn't said anything about me being with my friends for the last two days—maybe because there was no need, since Mama was gone—still, I could tell she disapproved.

"Let's do that play," Vanessa said, as soon as we all sat down. "Almay, we'll do that play Missy's mama wrote, the patriot one. You have a great voice. And Missy, you know a little piano, right?"

I nodded. "A little. I don't know if I can play all Almay's songs, though."

Almay frowned. "How come?"

"How come, what?" Vanessa said.

"How come you want to do that play? I get all the best parts in it."

Vanessa just shrugged.

We were quiet for a while. And then Almay said, "I don't miss him that much, you know. I mean, he scared me, sort of."

"He scared me, too," I said, relieved that we were finally talking about it.

"You know what's weird, though?" Almay said.

We both looked at her.

"He's *dead*," she said. "And I could be dead, too."

"Yeah," Vanessa said. "I know. I keep thinking that, too."

"And he's a kid," I said. "Was a kid."

"I know," Almay said. "Kids don't die. Except they do."

Yes. Dead. Gone. Not like how people go away, but then they come back. This was *dead*. Forever.

And I hadn't even liked him.

"Remember what he said about taking you to see a dead man?" I said. "Was there really a dead body?"

Almay shook her head. "Un-uh," she said. "I went and looked that day. Uncle Peach came with me. We looked up and down that creek. No dead body. Just some big logs, and once we thought we saw a gator."

"He was probably just making that up to get you to come with him," Vanessa said.

Almay sighed. "My mama says he's in heaven."

"Probably," Vanessa said. "'Cause he was a kid."

"If there *is* a heaven," I added.

They both just looked at me.

"Or a God," I said.

"Missy!" Vanessa said, sounding shocked.

I just shrugged. "Well, you have to think about it, right?"

"*I* don't think about it," she said. She stood up. "Come on." She went over to my desk. "Let's get paper and pencils and stuff and work on our play. Missy, do you still have a copy of it?"

I nodded. "In my shoe box. In the closet."

"Like you can find anything in that mess," Almay said.

"It's not a mess," I said. "It's organized chaos, my mama says." I got up and opened the closet door. I hadn't been in there since before I got sick, and I had to push aside a stiff bathing suit, some rolled-up socks and beach towels, flip-flops, and sandals, all of them in a heap.

Well, maybe Almay was right. It was a mess. But my box with my secret notebooks and stuff was there, nice and neat, like always, against the wall on the left side. Nothing messy about that.

I pulled it out. I frowned down at it. Now, that was funny. There was something there, something strange, something that I didn't remember putting there. It was a little package, rolled up in a white cloth, and I lifted it out.

I unrolled it. And sucked in my breath. I let out a little squeak.

"What?" Almay said.

I could feel a tight knot rising up in my throat.

I held the thing out, flat on my palm, my hand shaking. I couldn't even speak.

Almay and Vanessa crowded close to me, leaning over my shoulder.

"Oh, wow!" Vanessa breathed. "Yuck-o."

"How did it get there?" Almay whispered.

"Did you put it there?" Vanessa asked. "Did you put it there and forget?"

I shook my head, still not able to say a word.

"It didn't fly away," Almay whispered.

A bird. It was a bird. A stiff, dead little bird corpse, a mockingbird with a broken wing. It was wrapped carefully round and round; like a baby, it was wrapped. In one of Mama's handkerchiefs.

Nineteen

So here's the funny thing. You might think that things couldn't get any worse. And they couldn't. Well, maybe they could. But they didn't. They didn't get much better, but they didn't get worse, either. And the reason that things were sort of all right, was my friends. We just spent days doing silly stuff, making plans for the next school year, trying to work on our play, nothing important at all. We didn't talk about boys. Vanessa never even mentioned Matthew Winkler again, and I didn't have to make up any stories about the nonexistent boy at the hotel. We had a little quiet burial for the bird, and we didn't talk about it anymore nor how it might have gotten into my closet. We especially didn't talk about Mama and we didn't talk any more about Jordie. And at night, when I was alone and in bed, I tried not to think about those things, either. I especially tried not to think about Mama, tried hard not to picture what was happening to her, not to worry about if there were bars on her windows and if she could see the sky and the birds, not to think anything at all about what a mental hospital might be like. I just read till I fell asleep.

Another good thing was that Mimi kind of left me alone. She actually took to being in the kitchen with Geneva some, helping to shell beans or wash vegetables. And though Geneva was her usual grumpy self, she didn't seem any worse with Mimi around. It seemed that maybe they had made peace for some reason—maybe both of them were just waiting for Mama to come home.

Finally, one day Almay and Vanessa and I decided to get to work seriously on that play of Mama's, *The Patriots*. We went over the script and cut some of the music that Mama had written. It was Almay who thought of it, and she's not usually the one with the ideas. But she said that Mama's songs were too sad—nice, but sad. And I think she was right.

Then we added stuff, poems and some skits that we wrote. Vanessa wanted to include parts for all the little kids in the neighborhood, including the little Potts kids and the Montanas. That was fine with me, because by then the three of us were getting kind of bored with just each other's company.

My part was to write the songs. I'm not terrific at song writing, not anything nearly as good as Mama, but I did come up with some simple things. My favorite and best was one about a farmer and all his animals. Sometimes, when I was fiddling around at the piano, Mimi came and sat in the room, and though she made me uncomfortable sitting there listening, she didn't say anything bad. Though she didn't say anything nice, either.

We had planned to put on the play on a Wednesday afternoon, because some of the dads only worked a half day on Wednesday, and we wanted all the neighbors to come. Still, I wasn't completely happy with it. I thought we needed more than just songs and skits. When Mama was here, she had such wonderful ideas. Like in the first *Patriots* play, she somehow managed to create a moon, a huge ball with light bulbs inside that hung from the living room ceiling. It turned slowly as we sang about the moon over the sailing ships. That was the kind of fun thing that was missing. But Almay and Vanessa, they thought it was just fine.

It was late one broiling-hot afternoon, and the three of us were on the side porch, the ceiling fans going, sending out a little bit of a breeze, but not enough to really cool things off much. We had been taking turns making tickets for the play and were getting ready to sell them. I had made a bunch of them, and Vanessa had done a bunch, and now Almay was doing hers. Hers were way different from mine and Vanessa's. Mine were just plain, the time and date and name of the play. But Almay's were all flowery and in bright crayon, with designs all over. I have to say, I felt a little jealous. It seems sometimes that Almay has all the talents. She's good at art, and she's great at singing, and she had the first boyfriend of any of us. Even if he was a . . . well, Geneva says I mustn't speak ill of the dead, not even think it. So I won't think about what a jerk he was.

After a little while, Almay looked up from coloring a ticket. "*The Patriots* is kind of a boring name, isn't it?" she said.

Vanessa just grunted. She was in her favorite cooling-off position, lying flat out on the porch floor, her hand trailing over the side, looking a lot like a rug. "Whatever," she muttered.

"The name's OK," I said. "It's the play that's boring."

"Maybe it should be *Summer Days,*" Almay said. "How does that sound?"

"Hmm," Vanessa said.

"What's the difference?" I said. "*Summer Nights, Summer Days, Patriot Days,* it's all the same. It's just boring, though."

"Our theme isn't boring, all patriotic and stuff," Almay said. "I like it."

"And your songs aren't boring," Vanessa said, turning her head to me. "I like the one about the farmer."

I did, too.

"I like all the different animals you have in it," Almay said.

"Yeah," I said. And just like that, something came to me—began coming to me—an idea! "Wait a minute!" I said. "I have an idea."

"Uh-oh," Almay said.

I was in the swing, and I twisted the swing around to look at both of them. "Yeah, we change the name," I said. "Change it to *Summer Daze*—you know—*d-a-z-e*. And then we do something really, really silly!"

Almay just made a face at me.

"I mean it. Animals! Look!" I slid off the swing and picked up the song sheet that I had written, "Songs of the Farmyard." "See?" I said. "We get each little kid to bring in an animal. So instead of just singing about the farmyard— they could sing and then bring in the animals that a farmer would have."

"Oh, right," Almay said. "We're doing this in your living room, remember? Where the piano is? I can just see a cow walking in your front door."

"Or a pig," Vanessa said, not looking up from her place on the floor. "Oink, oink."

"Go ahead, laugh," I said. "But just picture it. Each new verse, another little kid comes trotting out with an animal. We can have kittens and dogs, and it wouldn't be hard to get chickens, and I bet Almay could get that peacock. They wouldn't be too messy in the house."

Neither of them said anything. Almay was still squinting up her eyes at me.

"So?" I said. "You two have a better idea?"

Vanessa struggled to a sitting-up position. "Well, maybe it would be fun," she said. "I could bring my guinea pig. I bet Gordon would like to get out for a change. And maybe my grandma will lend me Petey, her parakeet."

"Just don't let Almay's mama see it," I said.

Almay grimaced. "My mama still thinks the reason you got sick and your grandma came and Jordie died is because of the bird," she said. "All three things she blames on the bird."

I made a face. "She doesn't *really* believe that?"

Almay shrugged. "That's what she says."

It couldn't be true, no matter what Geneva said. It was just a superstition. But then, what if she was right? Did that mean everything was my fault, even Jordie dying?

"Nothing more bad will happen, though," Almay said. "That's what my mama said. Because bad things happen in threes."

Only it wasn't three. It was four. Almay had forgotten about Mama going away. But that couldn't be my fault, could it? That worried me sometimes, especially lately, because Daddy wouldn't let me go visit Mama at the hospital. He said the doctors thought Mama would be better with no visitors but him. So that must mean I might make Mama worse.

I pushed those thoughts aside.

"Daddy has a store cat," I said. "But it never leaves the store."

"Give it a day out," Vanessa said. "Would he let you?"

I nodded. "I think so."

"Uncle Peach has a dog," Almay said.

"And what about the peacock, Almay?" I said. "Can you get it? Remember how you used to take it for walks when you were little? It followed you around like a pet."

"Yeah," Almay answered. "I just put a string around its neck. It's still down the lane. Uncle Peach feeds it. But we're going to bring them in the *house*? You sure?"

I made a face. That was a worry. Still. I shrugged. "It's just going to be for ten minutes or so," I said. "The part with the animals, anyway."

So for the rest of the afternoon, we talked and planned out our play and figured out what animals we needed. Almay said she could even get a horse. Until I said, "In the house?"

Then, after our plan was finished and written out, we went up and down the street, selling tickets. Only, we decided after just one or two houses, that maybe it wasn't a good idea to *sell* tickets—because no one wanted to pay for them. Also, I knew Mama and Daddy—well, Daddy anyway, and probably Geneva, too—would have a fit if they knew we were taking money from neighbors.

So instead, we handed out tickets, and then, when we were finished with our block and the neighborhood, we went down the lane and handed out the tickets there. Almay said none of the lane people would want to come, but I thought we should at least invite them. I figured that since we were borrowing their dog and peacock, it would be polite to ask. And if they didn't want to come, that was all right, too.

Everything was in readiness. We would rehearse once more with the kids on Tuesday—and bring the animals on Wednesday. That meant less than a week to go.

By then it was almost supper time, and Almay and Vanessa went on home, and I went back up the lane to the house alone. I was surprised to see Daddy there already, sitting on the porch swing.

"Hey!" I said, jumping up the porch steps. "You're home early."

Daddy patted the swing beside him. "Come sit," he said. "I have some news for you."

"News?" I said, and found that my hands suddenly began that shaking business they had been doing lately.

"Uh-oh."

"Not, '*uh-oh*,'" Daddy said. "Good news. Come here."

I went and sat beside him, but I tucked my hands under me to hide the shaking. I was pretty sure Daddy wouldn't lie to me, but I didn't really trust that whatever was coming was good news.

"Your mama's coming home," Daddy said, putting an arm around my shoulder and pulling me close to him.

I turned to look at him.

He looked straight back at me. He nodded. "She is," he said, smiling.

She was? She *is*? I thought of a million things I wanted to say. Questions and thoughts tumbling over each other inside my head. Was she better? Was she still crazy? Was she—was she normal? Herself? How much had she changed? Had she changed at all? But what I blurted out when I could finally speak was just one word: "When?"

"Sunday," Daddy said. "But not to stay."

"Not to *stay*?" I said.

"No. Just for a short visit—three hours, about."

"But why?" I said. "If she's better, why can't she stay?"

"She *is* better," Daddy said. "But she has to get used to things slowly. See, she has to get used to life outside the hospital. She has to get used to being with people, with us."

"Oh," I said.

"You understand?" Daddy said. "That makes sense, doesn't it?"

I nodded. Yes, I understood. It did make sense. It did. But it scared me. Because if she needed to get used to life outside the hospital—how could you not think the rest of that? Like: what if she couldn't?

But I would not think that now. I would not. Mama was better. That's what I would think of. Mama was better.

Mama was coming home to us.

Twenty

For that whole night and the next day, I felt totally weird. One minute, my body was doing that trembling thing so that I felt like I would never stop shaking. And the next minute, I was so happy and silly, I wanted to sing or just laugh—at nothing.

Daddy was sweet, as nervous as I was, but in a different kind of way. There are porches that run all around our house on three sides, and Daddy had taken to walking around the porches, back and forth, from one side of the house to the other, back and around, back and around. Late Saturday evening when I came out, he put his arm around my shoulder, and I put my arm around his waist, and together we walked—and walked—and walked, neither of us saying a single word. We walked until it was dark, and the cicadas began sawing away, and the night creatures started buzzing, and still neither Daddy nor I said a word. And it was all right.

It was Mimi who talked a whole bunch. She had been

sort of quiet for that whole time Mama was away, but now she was suddenly bossy again, telling each of us what we should do and not do when Mama came home.

And Geneva, she had gotten grumpy. I mean, Geneva's always a little grumpy, but she became downright mean-tempered with me. She was so busy with special preparations for Mama's homecoming that if I showed up in the kitchen even for a minute, she shooed me out. So I wandered from place to place feeling happy and excited one minute: Mama was coming home! And then nervous and scared half to death the next—because Mama was coming home!

Finally, Sunday noon arrived, and I went out on the front steps to wait, going over and over in my head what I should and shouldn't do. Daddy said I should just act like myself, not to worry. But Mimi had given me a whole list of things I shouldn't talk about or do. Mostly, Mimi said, don't upset your mama! Like, I was not to come rushing out to the car, grabbing Mama, and asking a million questions. If Mama wanted to talk about the hospital, she could talk, but I wasn't to ask about it and I should let her do it in her own way and her own time. And I should *not* say, Welcome Home, because that would remind her that she had been away. Like Mama didn't know that!?

Part of me was irritated, wondering how Mimi could know what was right to say or not say. But part of me was relieved, too. Because no matter what Daddy had said about being myself, I didn't know what would be right to do. I mean, suppose I said or did something that made Mama crazy again? So to Mimi's list of things I shouldn't talk about, I added my own. I would not mention the bird, would not ask Mama if she had killed it, or if she'd just found it dead. I would not ask why she had put it in my box, wrapped up so carefully, as though it was a baby child. And I wouldn't talk about our play because that might remind Mama of times when she had been better and had written the play for us. And I wouldn't talk about the piano and how I was learning to play the songs and even to write them—though I was kind of proud of that—because that could remind her too, that she wasn't here to play for us.

So I just sat on the front steps, waiting. And thinking. And feeling my stomach doing flippy things. Daddy was picking Mama up at the hospital at eleven o'clock, so he should be home by noon—in about ten minutes—and then we'd have dinner. Geneva and Daddy and Mimi had planned the whole visit, right down to the minute.

Geneva had cooked up a whole batch of fried chicken, Mama's favorite, and mashed potatoes and gravy and biscuits, and a lemon meringue pie. The house smelled wonderful, and if my stomach hadn't been so tumbly and nervous, I would have been dying for noontime. But as it was, I was too nervous to even enjoy the smells coming from the kitchen, just kept looking down the street, waiting for the car to turn the corner. And when it finally did, I thought my heart would just thump its way right out of my throat. My hands, which for the last two days had become so jumpy, suddenly got crazy again, trembling so hard that I had to quick fold them together, twisting them hard the way I had learned to do.

I watched as Daddy pulled into the driveway, remembered how Mimi had said not to rush the car, not to rush Mama—and then—and then I jumped off the steps and rushed to the car.

Mama was already opening the door, not waiting for Daddy, who was coming around the car to help her out.

She stepped out and held out her arms to me.

I ran to her, ran into her arms, buried my face in her neck.

She held me close, close and tight. She smelled hospital-ish, but sweet, too, sweet like Mama, her skin tangy and delicate, that familiar scent of oranges. I burrowed my face deep into her shoulder, listened to the tiny thumping of her heart, smelled her warmth, felt her arms tight around me, rocking me a little.

"Missy?" Daddy said softly.

"It's all right, James," Mama said. "Leave her be."

Her voice was calm and quiet, not wild and up—not sad and dim. Not yet.

I held on to her for another long moment, then pulled away and looked up at her.

She was very thin, thinner even than she'd been before, and I could see the trace of blue veins showing in her cheeks, her collar bones jutting out, the deep hollow in her neck. But her hair was nicely combed and brushed and she was wearing makeup, her usual kind, and I could see she had applied it with a firm hand, not that wild way she does at times. She stood straight, too, her shoulders back, almost like pictures I had seen of soldiers in training, a different kind of way of standing than I had seen before. Had they taught her to stand like that?

I noticed that her eyes were shiny with tears, but she was smiling, and she bent her face toward mine, her hands on my shoulders, close enough to look right in my eyes.

"How have you been?" she asked quietly.

The words were very formal-like, the kind of words you'd say to a neighbor who you hadn't seen in a while. But she didn't sound formal or strange. She was just Mama, just regular Mama, my very own mama who had been gone forever.

"I've missed you," I said. I didn't mean for it to happen, but my voice came out kind of trembly.

"Missy!" Mimi said sharply, suddenly appearing at my elbow.

"Hello, Mother," Mama said. "Mother, would you help James bring my bag into the house?"

Mama sounded pleasant, but when Mimi didn't move,

Mama said it again. "Please bring my bag into the house. I want to speak with Missy. Can you leave us be for a moment?"

Mama turned me around then, her hand on my shoulder, and walked with me toward the back of the house, toward the garden. "Tell me everything," she said. "You were so sick when I left. But I knew from Daddy that you were getting better."

"I got better."

"I was afraid," Mama said. "Afraid because I couldn't make you better. I *willed* you to be better."

"I wanted *you* to be better, too," I said. "And I couldn't make *that* happen, either."

For a minute, I couldn't think what else to say, because I knew I wasn't supposed to talk about certain things, and I didn't even know if what I had just said was all wrong. But Mama took care of that by beginning to talk herself.

"I'm glad I went to the hospital," Mama said. "I needed that time away."

I didn't look at her. "Away from me?" I said.

"No. Not away from you. Just away."

"I was afraid you wouldn't come back!" I said. "Or that you'd come back so . . . so different I wouldn't know you!"

And I knew the minute I said that, that I shouldn't have. I was already breaking all kinds of rules. I was saying things that could make Mama crazy again.

"You don't need to worry about me not coming back," Mama said. "Not ever."

I didn't answer. But I was thinking, how did she know I didn't need to worry about that? How could she know that she'd always come back? She didn't even know when she'd have to leave again.

"I think things will be different now," Mama said, as though she knew just what I was thinking, as though maybe she had had the same thoughts. "I think I've learned a lot since I've been away. You know, that hospital isn't so bad.

There are other people there like me. I'm taking new medi-
cine now. And there were treatments. I know the treatments
have helped."

"Treatments?" I said. "What's that?"

"Oh, there's a name for them. But it doesn't matter."

"Was it scary?" I asked.

Mama nodded. "A little."

"I was scared when you were gone."

"I'm sorry," Mama said. "You know, I've learned something. I learned there's a name for what happens to me."

I just looked at her.

Mama nodded. "There is. And just knowing there's a
name helps a lot." She smiled. "I guess when it comes to my
head, there's nothing simple. But there are new medicines
now. And of course, the treatments."

"But will you get—you know—sick again?" I asked.

For a minute, Mama didn't answer. And then she sighed.
"The truth?" she said. "I'd like to say no; I won't ever get sick
again. But the truth is, I don't know. I don't think so. But I
don't know."

I sighed, too. "OK," I said. And then I said, "Let's go
inside." Because I knew Geneva was waiting, and I knew about
the carefully drawn-up plan that had been made. I didn't want
to mess things up, because no matter how well Mama
appeared to me at the moment, I had learned you never could
tell.

Mama and I were going up the back steps into the
kitchen, when Mama said quietly, "I'm sorry about your bird."

I stopped and looked at her. "Did you kill it?" I asked. Oh,
no! What was wrong with me? I was saying all the wrong things,
and I had promised myself not to!

"No," Mama said, shaking her head. "No, I didn't kill it. It
was dead, and it looked so sad, so pitiful, that I wanted to do
something for it. You were lying there hot with fever. I thought

it was one thing I could do."

"It's all right!" I said quickly.

"I thought I would bury it for you," Mama went on. "And I tried to wrap it up nicely. But then—then, I guess things got going in my mind. But I haven't forgotten the bird, that whole time in the hospital. And I wanted to tell you that I was sorry it had died."

"I found it in my box," I said, "wrapped up in your hand-kerchief."

"I thought it would be safe there. I know how you treasure that box," Mama said. She smiled slightly then, wrinkling up her nose. "I hope it didn't smell or anything."

"No," I said. "It didn't smell. Or anything." I couldn't help smiling back then. "It just got kind of flat and brittle."

"Yuck," Mama said.

"I buried it."

"That's good," Mama said. "Know what, Missy? That wasn't a crazy thing to do, to wrap up the bird to bury it. That was all right—though I shouldn't have left it in your clos-et, I guess. But other things I did were a bit crazy. I'm working hard at figuring out what's just—me, different maybe from other people, but me. And what's crazy."

I looked up at her, saw her looking back at me, and I sud-denly realized something. What she had just said was right. She did have to work at things other people just took for granted. Like, I've always known she didn't know how to be a regular mama. But it wasn't just being a mama that was hard for her, that she had to learn. She had to learn what was nor-mal and what wasn't normal. Like she had just said, she had to learn what was crazy and what was just—different.

And she—my very own mama—was very, very different. And right this minute, that was perfectly all right with me.

Twenty-one

I felt bad when Mama had to leave that day but not terribly sad, because I knew she would be back next Sunday for another visit. And then, who knew? Maybe soon, she'd be back for good. I tried not to get my hopes up too much, but it seemed pretty clear to me that she was better. She acted different, somehow—sort of clear in her head, direct with Mimi, even funny with some of her tales of the hospital. And maybe the best sign: she ate a whole lot.

Of course, on Monday, Almay and Vanessa had to hear all about it. I didn't tell them much—felt I had to hold some things tight inside me—but I told them Mama was better, and that maybe she'd stay better. I know they knew I was happy. It had to show. I couldn't stop humming and singing, and every so often, I broke into a dance. By Wednesday, the day of our play, Almay said she thought I might break out of my skin.

I just made a face at her, but she was right—I can't remember when I had felt happier and better.

Vanessa and Almay and I had set up chairs for the play.

The piano room has big glass double doors that open out into the hall, and we opened the doors and set up chairs both in the piano room and out in the hall. We had no idea how many people would come, but we were pretty sure that at least the mothers of the little kids in the play would show up. So we definitely would have an audience.

We used the dining-room chairs and the chairs that line the hall, and we brought in some of the ones Mama and Daddy used back when they played bridge or canasta, back when Mama was better.

Geneva fussed a bit at the mess we were making, but even so, she agreed to make sweet tea and cookies for everyone. She even iced the cookies with red, white and blue icing to fit our theme. I had the feeling that she was just happy to see me occupied and out from under her feet. And Mimi—I could hardly believe it, but she actually helped with the chairs. It was her suggestion that we open up the doors to have extra room in the hall. She didn't help with *moving* the chairs—of course—but she did direct us. Naturally, we hadn't said anything about the animals, not to anyone but the kids in the play. I knew Geneva would have a fit about chickens in the house and the peacock, and Daddy raised his eyebrows when I went and got the store cat, Sammy, though he didn't ask why. But we definitely decided against Petey, the bird. No sense getting Geneva all het up again. And to tell the truth, even though I didn't believe that superstition, I felt better not testing it myself.

At just before three o'clock, the little kids started arriving. There were the Potts twins, James and Arthur, and the three little Montana girls, and Georgie and Jackie from the street behind ours, a brother and sister who look just like twins even though one is three and one is four. And at the last minute, we got some of the Henry kids. We had tried to coax all eight of them to be in our play, even though they have the reputation for being the worst and wildest kids in the neighborhood. But we asked because we figured they'd be really good at holding on to the animals, since they're always toting around dogs and cats and raccoons and rabbits and any other animal they can catch. But only Eddie and Ginny Henry showed up. The others were busy with tennis lessons at the country club, Eddie said. When I told Geneva, she said they were probably busy setting the clubhouse on fire. And Mimi, who had met them at church, sniffed and said they were probably too busy cheating the other kids.

But we finally had all the kids lined up in the backyard, out of sight of anyone inside the house. The animals we had put way in the back behind the shed, in the care of the oldest Henry kid, Eddie, who was eight, and his next oldest sister, Ginny, who was six and had brought along her own rabbit. That meant we had to change the song a little and add a verse about a rabbit, but that wasn't hard to do.

While Almay and I were in charge of the kids and the animals, Vanessa was being hostess and seating people as they came. Every few minutes, she'd come running through the house and out the back door to announce who had come. And there were lots! Dr. Potts had come, and Mrs. Potts, and both Mr. and Mrs. Montana, and Mr. Henry and the really, really old Maguire sisters from around the corner, and just lots of people! Vanessa counted, and by three-thirty, starting time, there were twenty-seven grown-ups.

We were almost ready to start, when we saw Uncle Peach coming up the lane. He was all dressed up, wearing black, shiny pants and a freshly ironed white shirt. He crossed the back lawn and came up the steps, took off his straw hat, and wiped his bald head with a bandanna. "Oh, it's a mighty hot day," he said.

"Uncle Peach!" Almay cried, grabbing his hand. "The play is in the front parlor, the piano room. Come on!"

"No, no, no," he said softly, pulling his hand out of hers. "Got to rest a bit first." He leaned back against the railing.

"But we're almost ready to start," Almay said.

"You can start without me," he said. He turned to me. "I hear your mama's a bit better," he said.

"Yes," I said. "Thank you." And I suddenly remembered the herbs he had given Almay for me to give to Mama, such a long time ago, and I hoped he wouldn't ask about them.

"You ready, Missy?" Almay asked.

I looked at the little kids all lined up. There was just one problem. Earlier, the three little Montana girls had suddenly gotten stage fright, and the only way we could calm them was with cookies. But of course, we couldn't give cookies to them without giving cookies to everybody. So now, practically every single kid's face was covered with red, white, and blue icing— all but for Georgie and Jackie who wanted to "save" their cookies and were clutching them tightly in their hot, sticky hands.

Well, I wasn't about to start washing faces—or hands.

I called across the yard to Eddie who was still behind the shed. "You going to be ready when we call you?" I said.

"We're ready now!" Eddie called back.

Ginny, his sister, yelled "Ouch! Quit it!"

"I'm not doing anything!" Eddie yelled.

"Well, don't!" I yelled back. "We'll call you in five minutes."

I turned to Almay. "OK?" I said.

"OK," she said.

"Let's go, kids!" I said.

We started our march around the house, the little kids banging on their pots and pans, and Almay blowing a marching tune into this little kazoo thing she has. It was supposed to be "Three Cheers for the Red, White, and Blue." But it didn't sound like much of anything but noise. Still, the kids loved it, and the more they marched, the louder they pounded on their drums. Uncle Peach followed along behind.

I led the parade, around the house, up the front steps, through the hall, and into the big room.

There were tons of people inside! Daddy was there! Right away, all the little kids started waving to their parents, and I had to quick line them up, facing front and the piano, so they wouldn't run off to their parents. We did the song "Three Cheers for the Red, White, and Blue"—and with them singing it, it did sound like a real song. I played and the Montana girls sang "The Three Little Sisters," the one that Mama had written for Almay and Vanessa and me.

And then we did a short skit we had written about summertime and frogs. It was pretty goofy, actually, but it got a lot of laughs, especially when the Potts boys came out hopping and croaking in the little green hats we had made for them.

Then I played the piano, while Almay did her solo. She had chosen "When Johnny Comes Marching Home." It hadn't made me think anything in particular when we had rehearsed it, but now, when I looked up from the piano, and saw Geneva standing in the back of the hall, it was all I could do not to cry. Her arms were crossed under her apron, and the look on her face—well, it could just break your heart. Because Almay's brothers, Johnny and Hank, would never come marching home. They were dead, buried in the sea where their ships had sunk early on in the war. And as Almay's and Geneva's eyes met, I saw for the first time what they both must have been feeling. And I wondered how I could have been so dumb as to not think about it before.

And then it was time for the finale, "Songs of the Farmyard."

During Almay's solo, Vanessa had run outside, and by the time the solo was finished, Vanessa and Eddie and Ginny and the others were coming in the front door and through the hall, each of them leading or carrying animals.

First came Uncle Peach's dog, Pootsie, a big, lame, moth-eaten mutt walking between Georgie and Jackie. And then came the peacock on a leash, with Eddie leading it, and a huge, fat chicken that was tucked under Eddie's arm. Then came Vanessa holding Sammy, the store cat, and a cage with her guinea pig, Gordon. Following her came Ginny, hugging a bunny so tight it looked like its eyes would pop out.

All the grown-ups started laughing and whispering and pointing. Uncle Peach, who had come in with the kids, was smiling that gentle smile of his. I didn't dare look at Geneva. Or Daddy. Or Mimi. I just turned to the song sheet, "Songs of the Farmyard." But before I could get even one note played, Georgie began howling.

"My cookie!" he yelled. "Stop it! He's got my cookie!"

By then, Jackie, his sister, was howling, too. "Stop it! Stop it!" she yelled. "Give it back. That's mean."

I jumped up from the piano.

The peacock had grabbed the cookies from both kids and was calmly devouring them, as both Jackie and Georgie chased it around Eddie's legs, shouting, "Stop it! Give it back!"

The peacock kept its head turned away and gobbled the cookies, leaving not even a smudge of icing on its face. But in trying to get away from the kids, it had hopped-flapped itself round and round Eddie's legs, till Eddie was wrapped up in the leash so tight, he toppled over—and knocked over a table onto himself and the peacock—and set the chicken free.

Of course, Pootsie began barking, and that sent Sammy running up Mrs. Maguire's leg. Daddy jumped up to rescue her—Mrs. Maguire, that is, not Sammy. And it was only with the help of Daddy and Mr. Montana and Dr. Potts and some of the others that we got all the animals corralled and out of the house. And that meant that our play was cut short.

But that didn't matter too much, because by then, things were in such an uproar that I don't think anyone wanted any more anyway. The kids were tired, and some of them had climbed onto their parents' laps. Georgie was sucking his thumb, and the adults were talking and laughing. But most surprisingly, they were telling the three of us what a fine job we had done. Even Daddy didn't seem mad. He just shook his head at me as he swept some suspicious-looking stuff out of the front hall. And when I went to take the broom from him, he just said, "No. Go on in and enjoy yourself. It was really fun."

And when Geneva opened the doors to the dining room and presented everyone with tea and cookies, I felt a little 4better.

Vanessa and Almay and I huddled in one corner of the dining room, whispering.

"Was it OK?" I said. "Do you think so?"

"I think it was great!" Almay said.

"Uh-oh," Vanessa said. She nodded her head toward the living room.

Geneva was down on her hands and knees, scrubbing at the carpet.

I went over to help. Someone—I mean, some animal—had peed on the carpet, and Geneva was blotting up the mess.

"I'm sorry," I said. "Can I help? I just thought . . ."

Geneva shook her head at me. "You don't think nothing," she said. "That's your problem. You don't use your head."

But she didn't sound angry, just her usual grumpy self, and when she hauled herself to her feet, she was smiling at me. "I just wish your mama could a seen it," she said.

"You do?"

She nodded.

"Should we do it again when Mama comes home? You think it was that good?"

"It was that good," she said. "But *outside.*"

Twenty-two

On the night before Mama came home——
"For good," Daddy said— I went into the kitchen to find
Geneva. Mimi had gone back to Atlanta, chased away by
Mama on one of her visits home, so there was no need for
me to avoid the kitchen anymore. I needed someone to talk
to, to worry with. There was just so much I couldn't be sure
about with Mama coming home. I had asked Mama just that
once if she was sure she'd stay well. And I remembered what
she had said—that she couldn't promise. Ever since that
time, every time she came back home for a visit, I studied
her, wondering if I could see signs that she was better for
good. But of course, I couldn't tell. All I could tell was that
she was better for now.

But staying home? Would that make a difference? Or
would she get sick again?

I was worried. Even Daddy seemed tense. Now he was
up in his and Mama's bedroom rearranging things, trying to
make things perfect for Mama. And of course, that made

Geneva half-crazy because she had spent most of the day fixing up the room herself.

Geneva was standing at the sink when I came in, wiping at her forehead with an old rag. It was dreadful hot in the kitchen, and she was just finishing up with the supper dishes.

As usual, she didn't turn to look at me, though I know she heard me come in.

"It's October," I said. "And it's still roasting hot."

"What you expect?" Geneva said. "It's Mississippi."

I shrugged. "I want fall to come," I said.

Geneva bent her head and wiped the sweat off the back of her neck, running the rag around under her collar. When she raised her hand to her head, I could see the pink of her palm, the rosy pink, so different in color from the rest of her skin. I remembered how when I was little, I would study her hand, turning it this way and that, turning it from the pink side to the brown side, over and over, until she got tired of me and sent me away. And I remembered how I used to think that Geneva's hands were pink on the underside because she had them in water so much, so I used to wonder why she didn't take long, long baths for a long, long time to turn all of her skin pink. Because I thought my skin color was nicer than hers.

Remembering that, my heart skipped a beat, making a sharp little thud in my chest, almost a pain. I went to the back screen door and stood there looking out. How did Geneva ever manage to put up with me? She always, ever since I was little, let me be a kid, a strange little kid, maybe even a mean little kid who thought she was better than other people. But just a kid. She let me figure things out, touch her, feel her, look her over good, the way a kid has to do, to find out what the world is all about.

For a long time, I stood at the door, listening to Geneva behind me, preparing her tea while she wiped at the stove, getting ready to sit a moment. The only time in the day that she sat down was after all the dishes were done and before she went on home.

"What you doing there, Missy?" Geneva said.

I turned away from the door and crossed the room and sat at the table. "Nothing," I said. "Just thinking."

"'Bout what?" Geneva said, her back to me, still at the stove. "You fussing 'bout your mama coming home?"

I just shrugged. "A little," I said.

"What's to think about?" Geneva said. "You thinks too much."

I shrugged again.

After a while, Geneva came to the table and sat down with her tea. The chair cushion made a little whooshing sound when she sat—her own cushion, her own chair. I have never seen anyone else sit in that chair; not even Geneva's friends who come visit sit in that low, curved chair with the saggy seat. But when I was little, Geneva let me sit there, my legs swinging because even though the chair is low, my legs weren't long enough to reach the floor.

When she was finally settled, she looked at me over her teacup. "What are you up to?" she asked. "Why you sitting 'round staring at me?"

"It's not you," I said. "It's just that I wonder what you're thinking. About Mama."

"Don't think nothing," she said. "I done told you that a million times before. Thinking does a body no good."

"You do, too, think!" I said. "Everybody thinks."

"Not this body," she said.

"Do too," I said. "Like try this: try *not* to think about white polar bears!"

She frowned at me. "What you say?"

"I *said*," I repeated, "try *not* to think about white polar bears."

"That'll be just fine with me," she said. "Never give a thought to white polar bears."

We were both quiet a minute. And then I said, "What are you thinking about?"

"Thinking about drinking my tea and what a nuisance you are," she said.

"I bet you thought about white polar bears," I said.

"No," she said. "I ain't thought atall about white polar bears. Now what you want?"

"I was just trying to prove something to you," I said. "People think all the time. And when you try to *not* think about something—then you think about it. Like the white polar bears." I took a deep breath. "Or Mama."

Geneva just shook her head at me. "You thinks too much," she said. "That's for sure. And you thinks the oddest kind a things."

"So," I said. "What do you think about Mama?"

She gave me that look, and I quick said, "I know! You don't think anything. But just tell me this. Do you think she'll . . . do you think she'll be . . . different when she comes back?"

"'Course she be different," Geneva said. "We all different. You different today from what you was yesterday."

"That's not what I meant," I said.

"Lord knows," Geneva said. "Done told you that a million thousand times. What's the sense of wondering and worrying and doing all this here *thinking*? You tell me that. The Lord knows. He writes the book."

I sighed. "You believe in God?" I said. Because I had been thinking about that a really, really lot lately.

"What?" she said.

She said it so fierce-like, I actually scooted my chair back a little.

"What you say?" she said again.

I took a deep breath and tried to look innocent. "I just meant, do you believe that God—you know—*hears* you? Like when you pray?"

She kept her eyes squinted up at me, and I knew she had heard my first question. She pointed a finger at me. "If you don't believe that," she said, "then I's real sorry for you. Real sorry for you."

I looked away from her, down at my hands.

Geneva didn't say anything more.

I took a peek at her. She was just sitting there looking at me, big and still and stiff as granite. After a minute, she got up and went over to the stove, poured herself some more tea. She didn't come back and sit down, though, just stayed there, her back to me. I could tell she was really, really mad at me.

I hadn't meant to upset her. But how could you know these things if you didn't ask? And she had always let me ask dumb questions before. At least, she used to.

I watched her standing there, studied the way her hair ripples in waves along her head, then is snatched up and tied into that big bun in back. I looked at her feet, the heels of her slippers all run over, the backs broken down so that her feet hang out of them. I studied all those things, willing her to say something. Like if I looked hard enough, I could *make* her speak. Make her say she wasn't angry with me. But she didn't. Not another word.

"Geneva?" I said, after a long while, when she still didn't come back to the table. "I do pray. I pray for Mama. All the time. I pray for you! And I prayed for Mama to get better and for Mimi, even. I did pray for her. And then Mama got crazy and Jordie died. But I still pray. I just don't know if God hears me. I mean, how can you know?" I took a deep breath. And then—then I said it again. "I mean, how can you know He's even there?"

"You can't know," Geneva said quietly.

"You *what*?" I said, so surprised I could hardly get the words out.

"You can't know."

"But . . . but you said . . . ?"

Geneva turned to me. "You can't know. You can only trust and believe. It's all you can do."

For like a full minute, we looked at one another.

And then I had to say it, ask it. "Even though God took your boys?"

Geneva took a deep breath. "God didn't take them," she said. "But yes, even if He did."

I looked away from her then, out the window to where the mockingbird was singing its heart out in the magnolia tree, going through its whole throaty repertoire of songs. And I thought—maybe Geneva was right. Maybe God didn't take her sons. Maybe He didn't even want bad things to happen, things like wars and sons dying and Mama going crazy. Maybe He just gave us the world, and people of different colors and kinds, and birds and music, and left us alone to work it out ourselves. But that made me think that Geneva was wrong about one thing: God doesn't write the book. He maybe writes the beginning. But we write the rest.

I looked up at Geneva, saw her watching me. Her eyes had that warm, liquid look, the same as that day when I'd first opened my eyes after being so sick. And immediately another thought came into my head, odd and ridiculous, but one that I absolutely knew was true: I bet that God is a whole lot like Geneva.

"You been writing new music?" Geneva asked now, very matter-of-fact-like.

I nodded, surprised that she knew that one song was different from the others.

"Whyn't you go work on them songs some more? Some

of them is downright pretty," she said. "Write one for your mama."

I just kept on looking at her, still so surprised at what she had said, surprised that she had *said* it—about God. And surprised that she knew about my music.

She nodded at me. "Now, go on. Get to the piano."

"OK," I said. I stood up.

I started out of the room, but at the door I stopped and turned. Geneva was standing in the middle of the room, stock-still, as though something had just suddenly popped into her head.

I smiled. "Geneva?" I said.

She looked at me

"What are you thinking about?" I asked.

She frowned at me, looking uncomfortable—embarrassed, even, I thought. "Nothing," she said, looking away.

"Something," I said. "And I know what."

"You can't know," she said. But she didn't meet my eyes.

"I do," I said, grinning. "White polar bears."